Richard Carpenter's

Robin of Sherwood

THE TRIAL OF
JOHN LITTLE

by Tony Lee

Originally published in 2022 by
Chinbeard Books
in partnership with the
Richard Carpenter Estate
This edition published in 2023
www.chinbeardbooks.com

Layout and typesetting for this edition by
Andrews UK Limited
www.andrewsuk.com

Copyright © 2022/2023 Chinbeard Books
Artwork: Robert Hammond
With thanks to Lucy and Dennis Collin
Sub Editors: Harriet Whitehouse & Barnaby Eaton-Jones

Contents

1: Forest Shadows

'Can we hurry this up? I'm hungry.'

Friar Tuck huddled into his robe as he sat against the Sherwood Forest tree trunk, using his hands to pull the hood of his habit around his neck like a scarf.

'And I'm cold. Did I mention I was hungry?'

Little John, currently leaning forwards and peering through a bush, took a moment to stare back at Tuck with surprise, shaking his head as he did so.

'You just ate,' he reminded the Friar, who shrugged in response.

'I'm very active,' Tuck muttered sombrely.

Much, the Miller's son, sitting beside him against the tree, chuckled.

'You're very active around the campfire,' he said with a grin. 'Very active when you're eating!'

'Now don't be so cheeky,' Tuck turned to his companion as he admonished him. 'Because of that, you'll have no seconds tonight.'

'I never do!' Much indignantly exclaimed, looking around for support; his eyes falling on Marion, currently trying, and failing, not to laugh at the argument. 'He eats it all! You know this!'

'Well, I need to keep my energy up—'

There was a faint sound in the distance as Tuck spoke, and he stopped as, like the others, he strained to hear from what direction the approaching cart was coming from. Robin, slipping down from a branch above them, landed in a crouch, patting Tuck on the shoulder.

'You can eat when we're done, Tuck,' he promised as he looked at the others. 'After you, John.'

With a nod, John grabbed his staff, and, as the cart came closer, he pushed through the bush, leaving the outlaw's hiding spot.

The cart was a simple, one-horse affair; hessian sacks piled onto the back, and an old priest, tufts of hair sprouting from his cheeks giving him the look of a rather annoyed owl, pulled back at the reins as John cried out.

'Whoa there, father!'

As the horse stopped, John walked into the clearing, blocking the cart's way.

'You travel this road, you need to pay the toll,' he said, almost apologetically.

'You stop a man of God on his journey?' the priest asked, the anger rising in his voice, his face reddening.

'And you have our apologies for that, Father Jonas,' Robin replied, as he too emerged from the bush now, his sword Albion in his hand, the others following him. 'But you know the rules of travelling through Sherwood Forest.'

'Tell us the truth of what you've got in your sacks, and, apart from a small donation, you can continue on your way,' John added, although this was spoken to the ground, rather than to the priest's face.

'Lie to us though, and the cost is… higher,' Marion finished the threat.

However, before she could say anything else, Father Jonas raised a walking cane and aimed it at her, like a sword.

'Shame on you, Marion of Leaford!' he cried out, using all his years of public oration to make sure his words echoed through the forest. 'Threatening an old man!'

'No! I—' Marion reddened, looking at Robin for help. 'Sorry Father, it's just—we need—'

'I know what you need,' Father Jonas relented, lowering the cane and leaning back onto the cart's bench. 'I have two sacks of coin, Robin of the Hood. One is for the Abbey, to help them through the winter. The other is for the Sheriff's taxes. And I'm afraid to say that if we don't pay those, we'll lose our lands.'

'That definitely sounds like the Sheriff,' Marion nodded.

'And Father Jonas is correct. Kirklees Abbey had the same threat last month,' Tuck shook his head. 'Damn the Sheriff and his brother.'

He paled, making a cross and glancing nervously upwards at the realisation of his curse. Walking to the cart, Robin stroked the flank of the horse, soothing it.

'Then there's no tariff for you today, Father,' he said, ignoring John's surprise at this. 'I won't take gold from a man of God when he needs it to help the poor.'

At this, Father Jonas leaned forward, grasping and clutching Robin's hand.

'God bless you, Robin!' he cried. 'God bless you all!'

And, with a crack of his reins, he started his horse walking again, with John only just leaping out of the way before the wheels brought him down.

'Has the sun cooked your brain?' John now snarled at Robin. 'We're not a charity!'

'I know, John. But if we take the taxes from him now, the Sheriff won't care who has them,' Robin explained. 'Father Jonas will have to find the taxes all over again.'

'And that means all the villages will suffer,' Tuck added.

John went to protest once more but stopped as he saw that Robin, watching after the cart, was now smiling.

'Why've you got that damn smile on your face?' he asked cautiously, looking back at Marion. 'It's never good when he smiles.'

'Think, John,' Robin turned back now, already forming a plan. 'If we wait until after he's paid his taxes, and take them from the taxman instead...'

John thought for a moment, chewing over the words in his head before breaking out into a matching smile.

'Then the abbey isn't responsible for it anymore and won't have to pay it back.'

'Exactly.'

Much frowned at this.

'Can we do that, Robin?' he asked, unsure.

'Of course we can,' Robin sheathed Albion, walking to the bush and picking up his bow. 'If we're going to hurt someone, then our dear Sheriff, Robert de Rainault, is a far better target. Come on, let's move—'

He stopped, staring off into the forest.

There, just out of the corner of his eye, more shadows than figures— standing still, unmoving...

No, surely not. Could it be...?

'Robin, are you okay?'

It was Marion's words which shook Robin back to the present.

'Sorry, I was just thinking of something,' he replied, almost shaking his head to regain his senses.

'You went white as snow,' Much said as he stared up at Robin's face. 'Might have been that soup Tuck made last night. Them vegetables been hanging around for ages before he cooked 'em.'

'I can hear, you know,' Tuck muttered.

'You should be able to,' Much snapped back. 'Your ears are as big as your stomach.'

As Tuck and Much stomped off together, both arguing over the quality of last night's soup, Marion leaned in closer.

'You were staring off into that clearing like you'd seen a ghost,' she breathed.

Pulling Marion away from the others, Robin glanced back over to the woods, where moments earlier he'd seen… no, it couldn't have been…

'I saw my past,' he sighed. 'For a moment, in that clearing? I saw Dickon and Tom. I know, it sounds insane. But they looked alive, Marion. Just like they did the night before we first attacked Baron de Belleme's castle. When they…'

'Were they saying anything?' Marion pressed. 'Doing anything?'

Robin looked at her in surprise.

'You believe me?' he asked.

'Of course I believe you,' Marion smiled gently. 'Your visions have saved us all on multiple occasions and, more importantly, I remember what you said to us about remembering them.'

Robin thought back, remembering the end of that terrible fight; after saving Marion, defeating the Baron and escaping the castle and de Rainault's forces, Robin and the survivors had retreated deep into Sherwood. Finding solace in a bluff that looked out over the forest, Will Scarlet, good, strong Will, had said then that it was over, but Robin had disagreed.

'Our friends who were killed, they'll never starve, or be tortured, or chained in the dark. They're here with us in Sherwood and they always will be, because they're free.'

Tom the Fletcher and Dickon of Barnesley were still in Sherwood.

And Robin knew why.

'They were waving to me to join them,' he whispered, haunted still. 'As if my time was ending.'

'Well, that's just silly,' Marion scoffed, but stopped as Robin, his face filled with urgency, took her by the arms.

'Is it, Marion?' he implored. 'We've been luckier than most recently. The Hounds of Lucifer, everything that happened in Uffcombe… And even back at the start, fighting de Belleme when we were hideously outnumbered – I still blame myself for their deaths. They were part of what we were fighting for, we stood side by side… on that beach…'

Trailing off, he looked back at the space where the shadows of his friends had been.

'What if this is a warning, an omen of what's to be?'

'Then I will march down and block your way to the underworld,' Marion squared her shoulders, ready for a fight. 'You can't die, Robin. You just can't!'

Robin stared at the woman facing him, seeing again the reason he loved her so.

'It won't come to that,' he lied reassuringly. 'It's probably just tiredness.'

'Then say that like you mean it,' Marion replied, but Robin had already walked off, following the others.

'Robin!' Marion shouted after him, almost pleading as her words echoed across the now empty clearing.

'Tell me you're not going to die!'

2: Book Delivery

'It should be *my* land!'

'The hell it is! I've worked that land since I was a child!'

In the great hall of Nottingham Castle, Robert de Rainault, the Sheriff of Nottingham, lounged on his gold and green-painted throne, his boots resting on a stool to his right, and stared down at his half-filled silver goblet, wondering idly whether he could beat both these bickering peasants to death with it before someone actually bothered to stop him. In fact, the only reason he didn't consider going through with this was because he was wearing his favourite tunic; the red and gold one that matched his chain of office so well, and the thought of having to clean blood out of it, yet again, was a painful and long-winded experience.

Who was he kidding, he smiled to himself as he considered this, he wouldn't be the one to actually do it. And if the guards failed, he'd just flog them as well.

One of the unfortunate parts of being Sheriff was that sometimes, as little as he could possibly get away with, in fact, he'd have to umpire these stupid petty squabbles; nobodies who, for a brief moment, got to bask within his greatness, the cross-shaped arrow slit above his dais shining a single sliver of bright sunlight onto him, making him look like a God.

Of course, this wasn't accidental; he'd spent days working out the best position to place the seat of office, nothing more than a fancy chair and some decorations, if he was honest with himself. But even a bench draped with velvet could be a throne. It all depended on the worth of the ruler sitting on it.

And as far as de Rainault was concerned, he was incredibly worthy. More worthy than many, in fact.

More worthy than King John, though he'd never say it to his face.

The two men were still arguing, and the Sheriff realised he'd tuned out of their monotonous griping, watching another of the unworthy appear from the upstairs entrance, making his way carefully down the stairs. Sir Guy of Gisburne had slipped and fallen the last time he entered; de Rainault hoped it would happen again, but it wasn't to be this time. But Gisburne appearing meant something a lot more interesting than his current duties.

'Will the pair of you just shut up before I send Gisburne to burn the whole thing down,' he hissed, straightening up in the seat, leaning forward so that they could hear his words. 'It's obvious that you can't decide on who owns the land, so I suggest you both agree to gift it to the crown before Abbot Hugo gets his hands on it.'

He smiled. He'd once been told that his smile was his most winning feature, and so he used it here to ease any worries these peasants had. It didn't feel right though, so he changed it slightly.

A Lord didn't smile with scum.

'Don't worry,' I'll ensure that it's looked after properly,' he sneered.

Yes. That was better.

'That's unfair!' the first man complained, glancing at his opponent who, like him, was furious at this decision.

'I don't think—' the second man started, but de Rainault rose commandingly, interrupting his flow.

'I don't really care what you *think*,' he said as he walked to the side of the wooden dais and took the steps to the hay-strewn floor. 'Speak to the scribe on the way out.'

The two men stared at him in confusion.

He stared back impatiently.

'Now, gentlemen!' he cried out, tossing the silver goblet at the closest. As the two men ran in terror from the chamber, de Rainault looked back at Gisburne, standing to the side, a wrapped gift in his hand.

'Gisburne,' he waved his loyal knight forward. 'What do you have for me?'

'A book, sire,' Gisburne replied, and de Rainault winced. The man couldn't even emote properly.

'A book?'

'Yes, sire. It was delivered today. For you.'

'For me?' de Rainault was intrigued now, snatching the wrapped packaged out of Gisburne's hands. 'Then don't dawdle! Give it to me!'

Frantically unwrapping the hessian from the coverings, de Rainault stared down at the leather-bound grimoire in his hands. A book he'd waited months, if not years, to get his hands on was now in his possession.

'At last,' he muttered, scanning through the pages. 'Do you know what this is? No, you wouldn't, would you? This is the grimoire of Simon de Belleme. I've been hunting this for ages.'

'Are you sure you should be reading it?' Gisburne took a step back, making the sign of the cross on his chest with his hand. He knew very well of the dark powers of Baron de Belleme and had been in his castle the day he returned to life. Gisburne remembered the day well; he'd stood beside the Sheriff as the Baron, no longer dead, spoke to them of immortality while they stood terrified in the crypt.

'Somewhere in here is the secret of that damned silver arrow,' de Rainault, ignoring Gisburne's reticence, continued to read through the book. 'I'll use this to take it from "Herne's Son" and force the blasted thing down his throat.'

He looked up, noting that Gisburne hadn't left yet.

'Is there anything else?'

'Yes, my Lord,' Gisburne looked up at the door he'd entered through, as if expecting someone to walk through. 'I had a report from the gatehouse. A woman, Agnes Farrow, is in Sherwood and they say she talks of you.'

de Rainault closed the book, considering this news.

'What a coincidence,' he mused sardonically.

'My Lord?'

'I get this book, and she appears? I don't think God has that much of a sense of humour,' de Rainault replied, sighing as he saw the look of bafflement upon Gisburne's face. 'Farrow is a Witch Hunter. I've had to hold judgement on her cases several times, and they've never ended well. And having her around doesn't bode well for me, either.'

'Ah,' Gisburne nodded, although de Rainault felt that this pretence of understanding was mainly for show.

'What should I do then, my Lord?'

De Rainault wrapped the grimoire back in its hessian coverings, placing it on a table to his side. He noted that there were many lit candles beside the table, however, and picked it back up, in case it was to accidentally catch fire. This started another thought; one of curiosity as to who it was that lit these candles every morning – but as he progressed down that path, he saw Gisburne's simplistic, confused face once more, and sighed.

What you should do is learn to make your own decisions, you simpering idiot, he thought.

'Make sure she doesn't reach Nottingham,' he ordered. 'The last thing I need is for her to learn that I have this book.'

After a moment where Gisburne just stood there staring at him, de Rainault irritably swung hard, striking Gisburne's chain mailed arm with the package.

'Well go on then!' he shouted.

As if spurred into life, Gisburne nodded and left the chamber. Now alone, or at least as alone as one could be when you were a figure of such great importance, Robert de Rainault stroked the package in his hands, almost feeling the power running through it.

So, Agnes Farrow, he thought to himself as he walked back to his throne, calling out for a new goblet of wine. What brings you back to Sherwood?

3: Weapons Practice

The silent calmness of Sherwood Forest was currently being disrupted, as the newest recruits of the outlaws, nicknamed the Merry Men, proved their worth to the dark-skinned, black-haired and black-armoured man in their midst; his arms folded and his double blades sheathed on his back, he observed their movements intently, his years as a warrior giving him insights into their abilities and failings far better than any other in the woods that day.

One man using the wooden swords was Much, the Miller's son; he'd learned recently, and the hard way, of his lack of ability in melee fighting, and Robin had suggested he ask Nasir for some pointers.

Much hadn't expected to be lining up with the new people, though. Many of them hadn't even held a sword before, let alone use one.

Nasir, watching the contests, held up his hand; a silent order to stop their actions.

'No,' he commanded, his voice soft, melodious, his accent providing a slightly upturned lilt to his words. 'You hold weapons like children. I will teach you to be men. Again.'

'But I don't want to fight with sticks—' Much bemoaned, staring at his wooden sword rather than the man facing him, yelping with pain as his opponent's blunt blade clacked onto his fingers, causing him to drop his own weapon and suck on his now painful knuckles, glaring at Nasir as if this was all his fault.

'I see Nasir is being his usual, easy-going self with the new recruits—' John said as he watched the contests, sitting on an overturned log, Robin beside him. However, before John could finish, his friend had already interrupted him.

'Nobody can be mollycoddled, John,' he said sullenly. 'I want no more deaths on my conscience.'

John paled.

'Robin, I meant nothing by that—'

But Robin had already raised a hand to stop his friend, his other one rubbing the bridge of his nose as he smiled apologetically.

'I know, I'm sorry,' he replied, staring up at the leaves of the trees above him. 'I've not been sleeping much recently. And I keep seeing – well, let's just say I'm spending a lot of time remembering dead friends.'

'I know what you mean,' John watched as Much, finally having enough, tossed the wooden sword to the ground and stomped off. 'I do the same thing too, sometimes.'

'I didn't know that,' surprised by this admission, Robin returned his attention to John.

'Well, you've got the weight of the world on your shoulders and all that,' John forced a smile. 'Easier to just shoulder it myself, rather than add to your burden.'

Another yelp from the new recruits distracted Robin for a moment, before he turned back to his friend.

'You never have to do that, John,' he insisted. 'Even if I'm not here, then the others would always help.'

'What, Much?' John pointed at the now empty space in the clearing. 'He'd forget in an instant. Will would get distracted by *talk* of fighting and start discussing the best blade to knife someone with, Nasir would be the one talking *about* fighting, and Tuck would grumble about "why isn't it lunchtime yet".'

Robin laughed.

'There's always Marion,' he countered.

'No,' John's reply was forceful and final.

'John, she—'

'I said no, Robin,' John looked at his friend, and for the first time Robin saw the fear in John's eyes. Fear of what, he didn't know. 'No Lady should hear what my history has to say.'

'It can't be that bad.'

John rose from the fallen tree now, pacing as he spoke; the pent up, nervous energy spilt out into his words as he talked quickly and clumsily, as if trying to make sure he got everything out into the open before his brain realised and tried to stop him. 'I was bewitched by de Belleme for weeks before you saved me,' he said. 'Months, even. The whole thing is a blank to me, but I've heard the stories of what I did.'

Robin rose to meet him. 'That wasn't you,' he soothed.

John smiled, but it was a sad, resigned one.

'And yet it was,' he replied.

Robin went to continue this, but a commotion in the clearing caught his attention; Much had run back into the melee, but not to fight. Instead, he called Robin's name in a heightened state of urgency.

'What's up, Much?' Robin asked, walking with John across the clearing. The recruits had stopped training now; Nasir too watched the conversation with interest.

'There's a girl here to see John,' Much said excitedly, nodding at John as he did so. 'She says she's from Hathersage.'

John felt a sliver of ice slide down his spine. Hathersage was home, a place—

'Where is she?' he asked, shaking the feeling off for the moment. He could feel the guilt he always felt when reminiscing later.

There was a rustling in the bushes and, through the scrubland, Marion appeared, a young woman beside her. She was petite, slim and incredibly pretty, her long brown hair pulled back into a ponytail, the thick wavy strands threatening to break free at any moment. And, as her green eyes caught John's, his heart swelled.

Because John knew this woman, once a girl, well.

'Hello, John,' she said, her voice breathless with either excitement or trepidation. Immediately, John walked over to her, grabbing her, holding her off the ground in a fierce embrace.

'Rachel!' He exclaimed, letting her back down. 'As I live and breathe! What are you doing in Sherwood?'

Now with her feet back on the floor, Rachel looked flustered as she pulled away slightly.

'Looking for you,' she explained. 'I've… I've got bad news.'

John stared at her for a moment, unable to speak. As the moment lengthened, Rachel continued.

'I'm sorry, John. Your father passed away,' she whispered. 'It was quiet like, in his sleep. We're burying him in two days. I thought you'd like to be there, you know, to say some words.'

Robin placed a hand on John's shoulder.

'You should,' he said.

John nodded.

'I'm sorry, Robin, but I need to return home for a few days,' he replied, a little more formally than he expected.

'Of course,' Robin looked at Marion, who also walked over, grabbing John's hand.

'Whatever you need, John,' she whispered.

Nodding at this once more, giving the impression that nodding was one of the only things he could do, John looked up as Will Scarlet spoke from the edge of the clearing.

'Come on, John,' he said, forcing a smile. 'Bring your friend and let's toast your dad's memory over a tankard of ale.'

As John and Rachel walked off with Will, Much and Nasir, the training, now forgotten, ended. Now was not a time for fighting. Now was a time for healing, for being there for one another. Robin watched this, wondering whether Nasir was using this as another test for the recruits, a test of empathy for their fellow outlaws.

'We should go with him,' Marion said, jerking him out of his thoughts.

'What, to Hathersage?'

'He'll need support,' Marion held Robin's hand as she spoke. 'The death of a father is not something you just get over.'

Robin went to respond to this; he knew more than anyone how the death of a father shaped a person, but something to the back of the clearing, a shadow moving caught his eye, the raise of a hand – and without realising he pulled from Marion, running across the clearing, chasing the figure as, in the distance, he could hear Marion calling, asking where he was going—

'Get back here!' he cried out after the figure 'I see you – Dammit!'

Robin had almost tumbled off a cliff edge, the forest of Sherwood now below him, as the ground gave way to harsh stone. If he'd taken a couple of steps more, he too would have gone off.

But if there was no way to escape here, where had the figure gone?

'Robin,' Marion, out of breath, finally caught up with him. 'You're scaring me.'

Robin turned back to her, his eyes blazing as he grabbed her arms, staring at Marion as he spoke.

'Did you see him?' he asked, his voice high and desperate. 'Tell me you saw him!'

'Who?' Marion looked around, trying to see the figure Robin was talking about. But Robin pulled away, staring out across the forest.

'My father,' he whispered. 'Ailric of Loxley.'

There was a moment of silence as Marion tried to comprehend what Robin had just said.

'He was right here,' Robin pointed at the rock beneath their feet. 'He raised his hand...'

He shook his head, sighing.

'Perhaps I do need a break,' he admitted as Marion once more took his hand in hers.

'You've been thinking about dead friends,' she soothed. 'John's father just died...'

She trailed off as the slightest of smiles appeared on Robin's face.

'Where would I be without you, Marion?' he asked with genuine sincerity. Marion considered the question, weighing up the worthiest answer to this.

'Drunk in a tavern, most likely,' she replied honestly. 'Come on, let's tell John we're going with him for moral support. I think some time away from Sherwood would do you good.'

'I will. But I need to go somewhere first,' Robin looked out across the forest one last time. The image of his father, his hand raised, was still burned onto his retina. There had to be something more here.

'Herne?'

Robin nodded.

'I need to be sure these visions mean nothing,' he said, before kissing Marion lightly and leaving her alone on the Sherwood cliff.

4: The Ridge Way

They started the journey to Hathersage later that day. Robin had returned to the camp an hour later, claiming that Herne wasn't to be seen, but his haunted eyes revealed a different answer to Marion's question, one Robin wouldn't answer until later that day.

John rode on a two-horse cart, Rachel beside him; Marion rode a pale steed once owned by the Sheriff himself, and Robin held back, riding alongside the surprising fifth member of the group.

'You know, I'm perfectly capable of doing this on my own,' John shouted back to Marion, doing a poor job of hiding his irritation at the situation.

Marion, knowing there was more going on in John's head right now than just travelling arrangements, smiled softly at him as she replied. 'I'm sure you are. But you're family, and we wanted to be there for you. Isn't that right, Robin?'

She looked back at Robin, staring off into the forest to his right.

'Robin!'

Jerked back to the conversation, Robin glanced back at Marion and smiled weakly.

'What? Yes. Family,' he replied, almost as an afterthought.

'Well you're a bundle of bloody joy,' John muttered. 'Herne tell you off, did he?'

Robin shook his head, his attention diverting once more to the woodlands.

'I couldn't find him,' he replied again, his voice once more hinting at more than an empty cave. 'It was almost like he was afraid to speak to me. Hiding from me. Anyway, I'm here now.'

'For how long?' Marion, concerned, asked.

'As long as it takes,' Robin smiled, and this time, it felt more genuine.

John snorted, glancing back at the fifth member of the procession.

'Well, I can understand you and Marion being here for me, but why is he here?' he muttered.

'I protect you,' Nasir replied, his soft, Middle Eastern lilt making it sound like this was the most obvious thing in the world.

'I don't need protecting, Nasir,' John muttered, his face darkening.

'I know,' Nasir replied confidently. 'Because I am here.'

'No, that's not – oh, God's teeth, Robin!' John turned to Robin, his expression one of desperation. 'Surely I'm not the only one—'

'Look, Nasir wanted to give you moral support as well, John,' Robin replied before he could go any further.

'Also, there is pit fight in Chesterfield I enter,' Nasir added.

'And there's a pit fight he wants to play in,' Robin repeated.

'In Chesterfield,' Marion smiled.

John turned back to the horses, fighting the urge to slam his own head against the side of the cart, just to see if blissful unconsciousness would stop this insane conversion.

'Fine,' he growled, thinking better of it. 'Just tell me Tuck isn't following. Or that Will hasn't gone ahead to kill some people, because it's a Wednesday or something.'

'We promise,' Robin was looking back into the woods as he spoke. Marion had noticed this and was about to speak when Robin looked back at her and smiled.

'I'm fine,' he said.

'You have that look again,' she replied, frowning. Robin wanted to reassure her, to tell her everything was fine, but he wasn't sure how to phrase it.

Because he could see Tom the Fletcher and Dickon of Barnesley in the woods, watching to him, waving for his attention, as if they needed him to follow.

He remembered the line he'd spoken to Marion, back in Sherwood, when he'd seen them in the clearing.

'They were waving to me to join them, as if my time was ending.'

Was his time as Herne's Son ending? Was this an omen of what was to come? Should he follow them, see if he could speak with them, or move on? And what of the shade of his father, seen earlier that day? An earlier Herne's Son; one who'd given everything in his service?

Deciding, Robin looked back at Marion, still observing him.

'Carry on ahead to Crow's Folly. I'll be with you shortly,' he said. 'I need to check something.'

Before Marion could reply to this, Robin jammed his heels into his horse's side and spurred off into the bracken beside the path, like a man possessed.

Which, in a way, he was.

***

Robin had been riding north for ten minutes before he slowed down, peering into the undergrowth, looking for some kind of sign—

'I ride with you,' the voice of Nasir cut through the silence, almost throwing Robin out of his seat in shock. 'Where do we go?'

'You scared the hell out of me!' Robin snapped irritably. 'Why aren't you with the others?'

Nasir shrugged.

'You rode into woods with death on your face,' he explained, once more his voice soft and devoid of emotion; this was a simple answer to a simple question in his mind. 'Why wouldn't I ride with you? What are you looking for?'

Robin reddened as he realised how silly his answer was about to sound.

'It's nothing. I – I keep seeing dead friends,' he replied. 'I saw them again just now.'

'Did I meet them?'

'No, they died before you joined us.'

'In battle?'

'Yes,' Robin thought back to that terrible day. 'The day you arrived, when you fired the flaming arrow into the lake with us? That was our memorial to them.'

Nasir nodded slowly, also remembering the day.

'Then they are in your mind. Your friends would have gone to Paradise,' he explained patiently.

In answer, Robin waved around the forest.

'To some, Sherwood is a paradise,' he said, realising how he must sound. 'Come on, let's catch up with the others.'

Nasir looked into the undergrowth, and for a moment Robin wondered whether he was trying to see the ghosts as well.

'And your dead friends?'

Robin smiled weakly.

'As you said, they're just figments. Nothing more.'

He took a deep breath, gave a silent prayer to Herne and started his horse back towards the path.

'Although, they seemed to wave me away from Crow's Folly,' he finished as the two outlaws made their way back to the path, and the route to the village, only an hour away.

If Robin had looked back, he would have seen three shadows there: in the woods, watching him.

Shadows that, if you squinted, could possibly have been similar to the faces of Tom the Fletcher, Dickon of Barnsley and Ailric of Loxley.

Shadows that, as the last rays of the day's sun broke through the canopy of trees, faded into nothing, as the forest returned to its regular, quiet self.

5: The Folly of Crows

The town of Crow's Folly was empty as Marion, John, and Rachel rode through it.

'I've never seen Crow's Folly this quiet before,' Marion muttered nervously. 'And today's market day, as well.'

'Maybe they think we're Gisburne?' John suggested, grabbing his staff from the back of the cart and placing it within easy reach. 'We rarely travel by horse.'

'No, John. Something's wrong,' Marion shook her head, a feeling of unease washing over her. Rachel grabbed John by the arm, turning his attention to her.

'John,' she started, almost apologetically. 'I just wanted to say you were always good to me when we were children, and I always thought we'd end up together. And, although it wasn't to be, I just wanted to say… I'm sorry.'

This said, she squeezed his arm and, before he could reply, jumped off the cart, running down one of the side alleys between the huts, leaving Marion and John alone as they rode into the village square.

'What did she mean by that?' John looked around the square, but Marion had already beaten him to the answer, pulling out her sword in readiness for whatever was about to happen.

'I think this is a trap, and she led us into it—' she started, but stopped as from the alleys and pathways that surrounded them, soldiers wearing the red tabards and armour of King John appeared. Their swords were raised, and several had vicious-looking crossbows that were aimed at Marion and John's heads.

'It's Gisburne!' John exclaimed, pulling on the reins, trying to turn the cart quickly. 'Quick! This way!'

'These aren't Nottingham soldiers, they're wearing the livery of the King,' Marion replied, lowering her weapon at the overpowering odds.

'That's no better option for us,' John hissed, now holding the staff as a weapon as he pivoted around, seeing the full number of soldiers around them. 'Dammit! We're surrounded! Where's Robin and Nasir?'

'Lower your weapons!' one soldier cried out.

'You can't have her!' John shouted back angrily. 'You'll have to get through me before you take Marion!'

'But we don't want her, John,' the voice was that of a woman and, as the shouting ceased, the owner of the voice emerged into the town square. She was middle-aged, perhaps in her late thirties, with her dark hair cut short, almost in a man's cut. She wore a simple grey dress, belted at the middle and worn under a brown, wooden cloak.

She gave the air of authority; from the respect that the soldiers gave her, Marion knew this was the person in command here, as the woman walked up to the cart, smiling calmly at John.

'We want you,' she finished.

'Who are you?' Marion asked from the horse and, for the first time since she appeared, the woman looked at her. Or, rather, looked through her; judging her, weighing Marion up in a glance.

'Well, I'm not Sir Guy of Gisburne,' she smiled. 'My name is Agnes Farrow, Marion of Leaford. I'm the chief Witch Finder for King John.'

Marion felt a sickening sensation as Agnes Farrow named her; as if someone was walking over her grave. This wasn't a random meeting. This was deliberate.

'So, you're here hunting witches?' Marion asked, putting on a brave face, hoping she could delay whatever was happening until Robin and Nasir arrived.

'Not today,' Agnes shook her head, looking back up at John. 'Today, I hunt sorcerers. This sorcerer, in fact.'

'Me? I'm no sorcerer!' The accusation flabbergasted John. In response, Agnes shrugged.

'Tell that to the people of Hathersage, John Little,' she replied. 'Tell that to the people you killed.'

'This is madness! John wouldn't hurt anyone!' Marion exclaimed, her sword rising unconsciously as she shouted angrily.

'Marion,' John's voice was soft, only a whisper.

'He's saved my life countless times, and the people he's helped—'

'Marion!'

John's voice cut through her speech, and Marion stopped, staring in surprise as he continued.

'She doesn't mean now. She's talking about de Belleme.'

'The Baron?' Marion felt like she was adrift, cut from shore, unable to steer the conversation where she needed it to go. 'He possessed you, John! You weren't in control of your senses!'

John sighed, dropping the staff to his side.

'That don't matter. When he took me, I—' he struggled for the words, '—well, I don't rightly recall what I did while under his power.'

'Well then, let me jog your memory,' Agnes interjected. 'Arson. Kidnapping. Murder. And that was just the first week.'

'Show me proof,' Marion, finally finding her footing, glared down at the Witch Hunter.

'I don't need to show you anything, girl. All I need to do is prepare this dark sorcerer for his funeral pyre,' Agnes Farrow looked back at John, speaking loudly for the soldiers and folk of Crow's Folly to hear. 'John Little of Hathersage, you have been accused of the crime of darkest witchcraft, and if found guilty will be burned at the stake until you are dead. Do you have anything to say?'

There was a long, silent moment before John spoke, his voice low and haunted.

'...No.'

Agnes went to reply but stopped as an arrow slammed into a wooden post beside her. Looking up, Agnes saw Robin, Nasir beside him, bow in one hand, and blade in the other.

'Then I'll say something!' he shouted.

'Robin! There's too many!' Marion cried out. 'Run!'

Strangely, though, although Robin was visible to the soldiers, not one of them moved towards him. They stood or sat on their horses still, silent, waiting for the order.

Agnes didn't give it.

Instead, she walked closer, watching Robin; or rather, his sword.

'What is your name, woodsman?' she asked.

'Robin of Loxley.'

'And where did you get that sword?'

Robin paused, glancing at his blade in surprise.

'Albion? I was given it.'

'It has been missing for years.'

'Herne the Hunter kept it safe.'

By now, Agnes had walked up to Robin, holding up a hand.

'May I?' she asked. Nodding, Robin passed her Albion. He knew it was a risk, but so was trying to fight his way through so many soldiers.

Agnes caressed the blade in her hands, staring down at it in wonderment.

'Beautiful,' she whispered. 'Albion. One of the Seven Swords of Wayland, alongside Morax, Solas, Orias, Elidor, Beleth and Flauros. It can only be wielded by the true of heart. I heard it was used in Uffcombe recently, defeating evil, the others destroyed and never to be used by Satan.'

Quietly, Robin nodded.

'That's correct,' he said, as Agnes passed Albion reverently back to him.

'And you stand by this man?' she asked, pointing back to John.

'I do, he stood with me that day,' Robin said, deciding to omit the part where John, as well as the others, had been possessed; this didn't seem the time to bring that up.

Agnes Farrow walked back to the square, rubbing her chin as she pondered aloud.

'To have a wielder of one of the seven swords stand as witness... It's unheard of.'

'John is innocent; I swear to you,' Robin called out after her. 'He was as much a sword in de Belleme's hand as Albion is in mine.'

Agnes stopped, spinning around to face Robin once more.

'And you can prove this?' she asked cautiously. 'You can bring me the Baron de Belleme to confirm your word?'

'The Baron de Belleme is dead,' it was Marion who spoke, but her tone was uncertain as she said the words.

'You found the body?' Agnes replied to Robin still, who now shook his head.

'No,' he admitted. 'And I haven't been back to check.'

'Convenient,' Agnes muttered.

'No, Robin,' John muttered now, staring at the floor of the cart. 'If she's right, then I should pay for my crimes. I don't remember what I did back then. What if I did these terrible acts?'

'You were possessed!' Robin exclaimed.

'If John Little was indeed possessed, then de Belleme would have used a spell to do so,' Agnes mused, now standing between the two men, glancing from one to the other as she spoke. 'Spells are in grimoires. Was de Belleme's grimoire ever discovered?'

'The Sheriff was looking for it, but I don't think he ever found it,' Marion replied.

Agnes nodded at this.

'So it is still in Castle Belleme. Find the grimoire. Show me the spell, and then I'll consider that John Little was possessed.'

'And what of John while we do this?' Robin sheathed Albion now, but still held his longbow ready.

'He will stay my prisoner, and shall have a proper trial,' Agnes straightened as she replied to Robin. 'Although if you tally too long, you may find that the judgement is made.'

'And who will be his defence?' Marion scoffed.

'God will defend him.'

'I don't think so,' Marion climbed off her horse, walking through the soldiers to stand beside John's cart, reaching up and grabbing his hand. 'I'll defend John.'

'Marion, you don't need to do this,' John whispered.

'What, and let you have all the fun? Don't worry John, I've debated worse with self-entitled Lords,' Marion laughed, still keeping up the appearance as she looked back at Agnes. 'Miss Farrow, may I speak to Robin before he leaves?'

At Agnes's silent approval, Marion walked over to Robin, moving close so that their conversation was kept between them.

'You need to find this grimoire, and fast,' she whispered.

'I agree.'

'Take Nasir with you.'

'No, he should stay here with you,' Robin looked up at the clearing. 'I don't trust these soldiers.'

'I don't either but remember that Nasir was possessed by de Belleme too,' Marion's voice had taken on a tint of urgency. 'If Farrow learns that…'

'She'll want to burn him as well,' Robin understood. 'All right, I'll go with Nasir. But I'll return as soon as I can.'

With a nod to Nasir, Robin spurred his horse around, and the two outlaws rode off into the twilight.

With everything back to a sense of normality, Agnes smiled.

'Right then,' she ordered. 'Trial will begin in the morning. Until then—'

'Hold on one moment!' Marion stormed over to her. 'You said you'd give Robin time to find the grimoire!'

'And I am,' as ever, Agnes's face was placid and calm. 'Usually, I'd start the trial right now. So, I suggest you spend the night planning your defence, Marion of Leaford… because tomorrow we begin.'

6: Night of Ghosts

Robin hadn't been to Castle Belleme since the day the resurrected Baron de Belleme had returned and tried to kill him, escaping the castle with his friends before de Rainault gathered his wits and returned for them.

If he was to talk about this to anyone, he'd state quietly that he was glad he never had to return there, to see the ruined battlements, or walk once more into the castle where he faced the Baron and his dark magics for the first time, his body sliced by mystical daggers, and then faced the Baron on the battlements, blasted off the walls by mysterious forces, and held in stasis as the Baron used his terrifying powers to launch the silver arrow directly at his heart.

If it hadn't been for the timely intervention of Herne himself, catching the arrow before it could strike, passing back to Robin for safe keeping and allowing him to run, he knew he would be another of the ghosts that lived here, screaming into the night.

Even now, months later, he'd wake up in a sweat late at night, reaching for his longbow, convinced it had once more burst into flames, or reaching out for Albion, hoping to deflect the hurtling missile, only to find them but memories, and only feeling settled once the bow or blade, the real ones, were in his hands again.

He'd hoped never to come back here.

As they rode through the main gate, passing under the rusted and broken portcullis, Robin glanced at the grassy knoll to his right; there, Tom the Fletcher and Dickon of Barnsley, barely known to him but still willing to risk their lives to help him rescue Marion, had fallen, fighting to the last breath against Sir Guy and de Rainault's overwhelming forces.

Sometimes, late at night, he'd wonder what it would have been like if they survived, and he had died; would Herne have chosen another son? Could it have been either of them? But usually Marion, realising that he was in one of his darker thoughts, would stroke his brow, whisper her love for him, and bring him back to the light.

But Marion wasn't here right now. And he really didn't want Nasir stroking his brow or whispering sweet *anythings* to him.

'I hate this place,' he muttered. 'And I hoped never to come here again, after we escaped.'

'Yes,' Nasir replied, staring around the courtyard too, his eyes haunted as he relived his own nightmares from that time. Realising this, and quietly berating himself for even bringing Nasir back to this place, Robin angled his horse around so he could place a reassuring hand on the warrior's arm.

'Sorry Nasir. It must be worse for you,' he whispered.

Nasir had been the Baron's sword arm since Jerusalem and the Holy Land; he'd been just as possessed and controlled as John had, but, unlike John, Robin hadn't rescued him before they escaped. Even now, months later, Robin didn't know how the surly, quiet Saracen had escaped after Belleme's death.

'Do you remember anything of the time the Baron controlled you?'

Nasir contemplated the question carefully. It almost brought a smile to Robin's lips, as Nasir always contemplated every question carefully.

'No,' he eventually replied. 'One day I am home. Next... I am here.'

He waved around the castle grounds, and Robin could tell how utterly unimpressed Nasir was with the situation he found himself in. And Robin understood well; to lose everything in a second, to find yourself with a new destiny, your family long gone, was a familiar one to him. Even when possessed by Lilith, Robin had still kept a little of himself inside, had witnessed his actions, while unable to stop them. And, at the end, when they escaped the castle a second time, he'd actively avoided coming back to check for proof of death.

'They never found the body, you know,' he said. 'Lilith raised him from the dead with the silver arrow, and after we gained it back, I never returned to see if he still lived.'

'You saw him, though?'

Robin nodded. At this, Nasir tapped at his head.

'Then he still lives. In here.'

Robin nodded at this as, climbing off their horses, they hunted around for a secure spot, eventually tying them to a collapsed cart by the wall before walking along the path; the gravel crunching beneath their boots was the only sound in the night.

'If he is here still, we must be careful,' Nasir pulled his twin blades out as he said this, believing these could protect him against the Baron's dark magic. Robin didn't want to dispute this, but at the same time, the castle felt different from the last times he'd been there.

It felt at peace.

'No, the air feels different, cleaner,' he sniffed the air, relaxing a little as he did so. 'If he lived, he's long gone.'

'With his grimoire?'

Robin shuddered. The whole reason for the return to this Godforsaken place was because of that.

'Let's hope not,' he said, glancing at the battlements. The sun, mostly hidden behind clouds, was now beneath them. 'It's getting dark. We shouldn't do this at night. Let's make camp and search at dawn.'

Robin stopped once more; a sensation, that of loss and impending disaster felt its way down his spine, forcing him to take a deep breath.

Nasir noticed this.

'You pause. Do you see ghosts again?'

'No, just memories,' Robin shook his head, forcing a weak smile. 'Come on, let's build a fire. It'll be cold tonight.'

***

'Could you please shut up? I'm trying to read!'

Robert de Rainault stared at the minstrel, currently standing beside the fire in the great hall of Nottingham Castle, idly plucking at his lute, with an expression of homicidal intent.

The minstrel, to his credit, realised quickly that the last thing the Sheriff wanted was a ballad like 'The Outlaw's Lament' and nodded silently, pausing his strumming and backing away hurriedly, tugging his forelock as he did so.

Now with the peace he required once more, de Rainault settled back into the gold painted wood of the throne on the hall's dais and had only just begin reading again when Sir Guy of Gisburne decided that perhaps this was a good time to bother him.

'My Lord, are you sure you should be reading that book?' Gisburne held a goblet in his hands, and with his nervous expression, de Rainault wondered whether Guy's fear came from interrupting his master, or because of the leather-bound book in his hand.

'What are you now, Guy, my wet-nurse?' de Rainault snapped, closing the book irritably as he looked up once more.

'No, my Lord, but we both know—'

'Both know *what*?' de Rainault interrupted, leaning in closer, lowering his voice to a hiss. 'Simon de Belleme is dead. I don't care what we saw. But if he isn't, then whatever dark magic he used to return is in this book.'

De Rainault turned, walking to the fire, picking up a goblet of wine on the table beside it, and downing it. He didn't do this because he was thirsty; no, it was because he didn't want Gisburne to see his face as he remembered that moment, back in Castle Belleme, where deep amongst the magical paraphernalia he'd mocked, the Baron had appeared, and spoken to him.

You speak of things of which you have no knowledge, he had said, emerging softly from the shadows. What is death, de Rainault? When does a man die? When his heart stops? When the last breath has left his body? When he rots – and if he doesn't rot, if the frozen hours stretch forever, his blood a silent river of ice, waiting… waiting… what then?

de Rainault remembered making the sign of the cross, and the Baron laughing, mocking his lack of faith.

You doubted my powers, and mocked my sorcery, he had finished. And yet you feared me.

But he had been wrong, for de Rainault didn't fear the Baron at that moment.

He wanted to know more.

He wanted to know how he too could cheat death, such as the Baron had. And here, in his hands, was the manner of his success.

Gisburne still looked unsure, and de Rainault grabbed his arm, pulling him even closer as he walked back to his chair.

'Think, Gisburne! Never dying, always powerful!'

If this was supposed to reassure his right-hand man, it did the complete opposite, as Gisburne pulled away, his face now an ashen white.

'You'd sell your soul for immortality?' It was barely a whisper, punctuated by the sign of the cross being made. At this, de Rainault laughed.

'Don't look at me like that, Guy,' he sneered. 'You'd sell your own soul for a bag of gold and a roll in the hay.'

The grimoire forgotten for the moment, de Rainault sat back in his chair.

The idiot's here now, I might as well use him, he considered.

'Anyway. What do we know about Farrow?' he asked.

Finding this more comfortable ground to stand on, Gisburne nodded.

'She came down from Whitby. She's been staying at the Abbey there.'

'And what would bring her here?' de Rainault stroked at his beard now and was surprised to see Gisburne's face light up with vicious malice.

'From what I heard, she's going to burn John Little at the stake.'

'Really?'

This was welcome news indeed, and de Rainault leapt up, standing, the grimoire clattering to the ground. 'Then we need to see that!'

'I don't think—'

'That's your problem, Gisburne,' de Rainault leant to pick up the grimoire as he spoke. 'You don't think. If John Little is going to be executed, then you can be damned sure that Robin i' the Hood and his band of merry miscreants will be there to try and stop it. We can cut off two heads at the same time.'

He placed the grimoire reverently on the throne.

'Besides, I'm the one who sentences witches in this county, not her,' he finished. Gisburne, grateful for the excuse to leave, exited quickly, leaving de Rainault once more to his memories and schemes.

The Baron had stated that the silver arrow was power, yet later that very day lost it back to Herne's insufferable Son.

But Robert de Rainault wouldn't make that mistake.

And Robert de Rainault would live forever.

7: By Firelight's Glare

After Agnes Farrow had made her declaration, the soldiers had taken John to a small crofter's hut at the edge of the village, almost as if scared to allow him to stay too close to the people remaining in Crow's Folly. Several families had already left, claiming family emergencies or, more often, simply taking their horses and leaving quietly.

John didn't blame them. There was a time he'd have done the same. And now he sat, alone, in the hut, staring at the hearth, the flames leaping up as the wood crackled and burned.

They'd brought him food, the soldiers that was, making signs as they gave him stale bread and water for dinner, symbols in the air specifically designed to ward off whatever "dark magicks" he had to bear on them.

John laughed at this. The only "dark magicks" he had was the ability to wield a staff like a Devil.

There was a faint knock at the door, and John looked up. He hadn't expected anyone else to come here tonight, and he seriously doubted he'd see Rachel again soon, so it could only be one person.

'John? Can I come in?' Marion's voice from outside confirmed this.

'No.' John returned his attention to the fire. He heard the door open and close, and felt Marion as she entered the enclosed space.

'Now you're just being petulant. And you really shouldn't be staring into the fire like that,' she muttered.

'Do you think it'll hurt? The burning at the stake?' John's voice was soft, contemplative as he spoke.

'It's not going to come to that,' he wasn't looking at her, but John could tell from the tone in her voice that Marion was likely trying to smile, to make her voice sound light and unafraid of what was to come. 'Robin will come back.'

John looked away from the fire at the mention of Robin's name.

'I hope so, I really do. But we both know he's been a little distracted of late.'

'Not so much that he'd leave you to die!' Marion was horrified at the thought; that John could even consider this unnerved her.

John, in response, let out a deep, mournful sigh.

'You should,' he muttered. 'I'm not the man you thought I was.'

'You're exactly the man I thought you were,' Marion came over now, placing a reassuring hand on John's shoulder as she continued. 'And more. Don't let Farrow get in your head. All she has are stories and rumours.'

'But what if they're not?' John looked up at Marion, and for the first time she realised his expression wasn't fear of the burning, but of whether the Witch Finder could actually be correct about him.

'Okay then,' she said, gathering up a second stool and placing it beside John, holding his hand as she looked at him, searching his expression for something more. 'Tell me what happened. Explain to me what you remember, so I can help you.'

John swallowed, nodding.

'I… Well, I was a shepherd,' he began. 'Used to enjoy that.'

Marion let out a laugh.

'You? A shepherd?'

'Among other things,' John shrugged, a little embarrassed. 'I made nails, too. Lived with my father in a croft like this, by the River Derwent.'

He settled back, considering his words.

'Anyway, de Belleme came through Hathersage on his way back from the Crusades.'

'That's a strange route to take.'

'Yeah. People said he landed at Whitby, made his way down one of the Roman roads,' John shifted on his stool as he remembered the moment. 'And I was shepherding on the moors when he passed.'

'And then?'

John's face darkened with anger.

'He had one of his women bewitch my flock,' he explained. 'When I ran after them, soldiers surrounded me. Next thing I know? I'm soaked, and Robin's wiping a pentagram off my chest.'

Marion nodded; she'd heard Robin's side of this story. Belleme had sent John after Herne's Son, and they'd met at a crossing in Sherwood, fighting with staffs. Robin had told her he only just managed to beat John, such was the larger man's prowess with the weapon, and he believed it was the power of Herne, added to the water in a goblet, that allowed him to bring John back, as the pentagram scrawled on his chest bubbled and cleared.

John, however, had the more practical belief it was good, honest Sherwood water that cured him.

'How long were you under his control?' she asked.

'Dunno,' John rubbed at his scruff of beard as he continued. 'But when I was caught? I had short hair and no beard.'

'I can't imagine you like that!'

'Neither can I now!'

They both laughed at the thought, a moment of lightness in the perpetual darkness. Eventually, the laughter faded, and John returned to his fire-staring vigil.

'It'll be all right,' Marion reassured. 'You're not the man you think you are.'

'I'm at peace with this, Marion. I've dodged death enough times,' John replied, eyes still glued to the flames. 'If I'm meant to pay for any sins, then I'll do it gladly. You never saw me when I...'

He stumbled on the words.

'Well, when I was like that.'

Marion shook her head, leaning back on the stool. There was something she'd never told John before, something she'd never intended to tell him, but now, in the dark of the night and soul, she felt it was right to confess it.

'Do you remember when we first met?' she asked carefully.

John nodded, smiling at the memory.

'Of course. You were travelling with Gisburne, off to become a nun.'

He looked up.

'Fat lot of good that did you.'

'No,' Marion shook her head, watching John. 'The first time I ever met you was at Nottingham Castle, when the Baron came to demand my hand in marriage. I walked past you to speak to the Sheriff.'

She leant closer once more, taking John's face in her hands, staring long and hard at it, before continuing softly.

'I saw your eyes,' she whispered with a shudder. 'And I can tell you now, John Little of Hathersage – Little John of Sherwood, that wasn't you.'

John pulled away, looking back at the flames as they licked against the side of the hearth.

'Thank you,' he whispered, and Marion could see he'd turned away so she wouldn't see the tears forming.

'Do you mind if I stay here for a while?' she asked, turning her wooden stool so she too now faced the fire, staring into its depths.

'Not at all,' John replied. And Marion smiled; for his voice was stronger, more determined. By telling him this one thing, confirming this one belief, Marion had helped John regain a piece of his soul, still uncorrupted by the Baron de Belleme, back.

8: Bad Dreams

Robin stood on the mound, the stones around him, sword in his hand. He'd ridden as fast as he could, and now he could ride no more. As the storm thundered above and the rain soaked his armour, he faced Robert de Rainault as he appeared with his men, knowing his time was over.

As ever, the Sheriff wanted the silver arrow, but he wasn't going to give it to him. He may die, but nothing was ever forgotten. He would not sell his life cheaply.

'It's here, isn't it!' de Rainault crowed in triumph. 'You're the guardian, aren't you, Ailric?'

No, wait, this isn't right.

The first crossbow bolt slammed through Robin's jerkin, sending a wave of intense pain through him; a wave immediately followed by three more, as the crossbow men surrounding loosed their bolts, each one slamming into his chest and back.

As he fell to the floor, he felt a wave of relief; his time as Herne's Son, the guardian was over, and soon a new guardian, a hooded one would come to—

Robin jerked awake, tossing his cloak away as he half reached for Albion once more – before focusing, recognising the walls of the castle, lying back onto the ground in a cold sweat.

A dream. It was only a dream.

Robin lay for a moment, listening to the surrounding nothingness. The fire was almost burned out, and soon the dawn would come, but there was no birdsong in Castle Belleme, because there were no birds here.

'You're the guardian, aren't you, Ailric?'

The line from the dream halted Robin. He'd met a guardsman, years after his father's death, who'd been there that night. He'd been young, only a teen, and the guardsman had no clue who the lanky, dark-haired boy serving his ale had been. In the tavern, he'd told his friends the tale of that night; how he'd taken the last shot and killed Herne's Son. Robin hadn't understood the story until years later, when he was an outlaw, and Herne had claimed him for his own, but the guardsman was long dead, killed in an argument with another soldier over a piece of cheese, of all things.

Why would he dream of such a morbid, change-fuelled moment? And why here, of all places?

Robin gave up trying to sleep, tossing a couple of pieces of wood onto the embers to restart it and, rising from rest, he strapped Albion back to his waist before stretching, yawning, and searching around the guardroom they'd claimed as their own that night.

What a desolate place you are, he thought to himself, as he scanned the ruined arches of the upper levels. Were you always like this? Where would you keep de Belleme's secrets?

The crack of a branch echoed through the pre-dawn, and Robin spun, Albion in hand.

'Who's there?' he hissed, peering into the shadows of the castle; there was a figure, watching him.

Belleme? The thought filled him with dread. He'd only just survived the last encounter with the sorcerer, the last thing he wanted was a rematch.

No. This was a more familiar figure, a man Robin hadn't seen since his youth. He wore a padded, studded jerkin, arrows in a quiver on his back. He had the same shock of dark brown hair as Robin had, but he was older, wiser, and sadder.

But then Ailric of Loxley had always been serious.

'Father, you're dead,' Robin closed his eyes for a moment, but when he reopened them, the shade of his father still stood silently in the doorway to the castle itself. Robin knew where the shade wanted to take him, and it was a journey he didn't wish to follow.

'Speak to me,' Robin urged. 'First Tom, then Dickon, and now you? What are you trying to say? Are you warning me? Are you waiting for me?'

'Who do you talk to?'

The words were from beside his right ear, and Robin spun, Albion ready to strike – only staying his hand as he saw Nasir, confused, watching him. Using Albion, Robin pointed at Ailric, still watching.

'There, the shade of my father,' he said. 'He's by that door, taunting me.'

'Taunting?'

Robin swallowed, nodding.

'It's the entrance to de Belleme's tomb,' he explained. 'It's where his body was, and where he tried to sacrifice Marion. He – my father, that is – he's waving me in.'

Nasir peered at the door, but Robin could tell from his expression that he saw nothing.

'Maybe he's helping you,' he suggested.

Robin shook his head, turning back to the fire, his back now to the shade of Ailric of Loxley.

'No, it's a trick of the moonlight. Nothing more.'

Nasir frowned at this.

'You have never denied your visions before—'

'These aren't visions, Nasir,' Robin snapped irritably, interrupting the Saracen. But then he sighed, sheathing Albion and holding a hand up in peace to his friend. It wasn't fair to take this out on Nasir; he had enough memories and issues of his own here.

'These are nothing more than wishful dreams,' he finished, looking back at the doorway.

His father had gone.

'Come on, let's see what my "father" wants me to see,' he sighed, taking a piece of a flaming branch from the fire and, using it as a torch, heading down the stairs.

***

Standing at the entrance to Baron Belleme's tomb, Robin found himself unable to take another step. However, when before it had been the Baron's own power forcing his muscles into paralysis, this time Robin knew it was simple fear of what was waiting for him.

'You can stay outside, if you want,' he whispered to Nasir. 'I know how this place must feel.'

Nasir answered this by pulling his two blades and smiling darkly.

Eventually walking down the steps, Robin had to will his legs to keep moving as he entered into the tomb. It looked exactly the same as it had the last time he'd been there; the pentagram the Baron tied Marion to was covered in cobwebs, his dusty sarcophagus covered in occult charms and wards.

Robin was about to comment on this to Nasir when a sudden skitter from the corner of the tomb turned his attention and sword to it; larger than a mouse, it didn't sound threatening, more like someone or something trying to escape, and Robin backed towards the wall, scanning.

'What was that?' he asked, almost as confirmation he wasn't dreaming still.

'Not a ghost,' Nasir said, hefting his double blades. 'I think the Baron is still here.'

Robin prepared himself for an attack, raising Albion. If de Belleme did attack, Robin needed to be ready.

But the dream he'd had, and the portents of the future given by dead friends and family now made him wonder if this was the moment Herne's Son was destined to die.

9: These Riddles Three

Robin steadied himself for an attack, waiting for the mystical winds that would blast at his body, or the knife slashes that cut flesh from a distance... but none came.

Eventually, he straightened, lowering the sword.

I live another day, he thought to himself. Thank you, Herne.

'Come out, we won't harm you,' he said.

'Why should I believe that?' the voice, a woman's, echoed around the tomb. 'You killed the master!'

'The master? de Belleme?' Robin glanced quickly at Nasir before placing Albion back in its scabbard. 'Look, I'm sheathing my sword. Who are you?'

'I'm known as Enna,' the mysterious voice continued. 'I know who you are, Robin of Loxley. And I know you too, Nasir the Saracen.'

'You were with the Baron,' Nasir stepped forward now.

'Aye, that I was. From the moment he landed in Whitby, my sister Lilith and I were his loyal servants.'

Robin shivered at the name Lilith. Even now, he remembered the enchantment he'd been under, and the thought of returning to it scared him.

'Come out into the light, so I can see you,' he said. From the shadows, a figure emerged; Robin had expected some kind of grizzled old hag, a gnarled knot of a woman with wispy dirty grey hair, but this was a young woman with long, curly hair. She was pretty, too, unblemished, apart from the burned and puckered socket where her left eye once was, now nothing but pink scar tissue and empty space.

'What happened to your eye?' he couldn't help himself and blurted out the question.

Enna smiled, stroking it.

'Guy of Gisburne burned it out,' she replied. 'He wanted the master's jewels. I escaped though and came back here – but I was too late. The master was gone.'

'I saw him here,' Robin replied. 'I hoped he was dead.'

'Oh no, Herne's Son. He's very much alive, somewhere,' she smiled, and Robin saw that several of her teeth were rotted away. 'Is that why you're here? To gloat over a corpse?'

Robin considered lying, but time was of the essence, and even though Enna had been allied to his enemy, she might be the only person who could help John.

'We look for his grimoire,' he explained.

'Is Herne's magic not enough for you anymore?'

'The grimoire is not for us,' now Nasir stepped forward. However, at his words, Enna's remaining eye widened, and her smile grew.

'And it speaks!' she exclaimed in delight. 'You never uttered a word when you were owned by the master.'

'I am not owned by anyone!' Nasir stepped forward, swords rising, but Robin halted him with a hand on his arm, and Nasir fell back into position beside him. Enna, watching this, sniffed, spat to the side, and grinned at him.

'Of course not,' she said. 'Good dog.'

'Don't be goaded into attacking her,' Robin warned, feeling Nasir tense once more. 'It's what she wants.'

Enna examined Robin.

'Tell me why you need the grimoire.'

'To save a friend.'

'With a spell?'

'With the truth,' Robin paced back and forth as he spoke, aware he was losing time here. 'He's being held by a Witch Hunter. The grimoire will prove he wasn't in control of his actions. Can you help me save him?'

'You, who tried to kill my master, want my help? You can hang!' Enna spat at Robin, waving her hands, creating wards in the air, before stopping as Nasir once more moved towards her, scuttling back into the corner with a cackle.

'Then we'll find it without your help,' Robin replied bitterly, looking at Nasir. 'Look on the upper levels. I'll search here. If you find it, take it directly to Farrow. Don't waste time—'

'Farrow?' Enna interrupted, an urgency in her voice. 'Agnes Farrow?'

'You know her?'

Straightening, Enna moved back into the light of the torch once more.

'Oh, I know her well,' she replied, turning to Nasir. 'And so should you, Saracen. You tried to gut her in Whitby.'

'Why?' Robin asked, but in return, all he got was a single shake of the head from the young witch.

'All you need to know is that I now understand why she wants the grimoire,' Enna replied cryptically. 'And it's not to help your friend.'

'So you'll help us?'

'I do not give things away freely,' Enna contemplated her next words. 'I don't want your money, wolfshead. But to gain my help, you must play my game.'

She walked to the pentagram, standing before it, mimicking the same pose Robin had seen Belleme do the first time he saw him here.

'I must be bested,' she explained. 'Three riddles answered. And then we'll talk.'

Nasir looked at Robin, shaking his head, but Robin shrugged back. What else could they do?

'Whatever it takes,' he said.

Enna smiled, the rotten teeth still unnerving in the torchlight.

'I reach for the sky, baring my fingers when I am cold,' she said, and Robin felt a shiver down his spine. He knew this riddle. 'In summer, you'll find me and my sisters in dresses of green, while in Autumn we wear gold. I am...'

'A tree,' Robin replied.

'You didn't hesitate,' Enna nodded. 'You knew this?'

'My father taught it to me,' Robin said, looking back at the doorway. Was this why Ailric of Loxley had appeared? To remind Robin of childhood games now defining a life in the balance?

'I am at the beginning of the end, and the end of time,' Enna continued with the second riddle. 'I turn victory into alcohol and finish every rhyme. What am I?'

Once more, Robin smiled. Another riddle, told to him by his father as a child.

'A victory is a win, and wine can be drunk, and if you are at the start of end?' he replied confidently. 'Then you are the letter E.'

'I am impressed,' Enna raised her arms theatrically. 'And now the last one.'

As she started, the wind built, and the flame at the end of Robin's torch flickered; the tomb glowed, new flames appearing in the corners of the tomb, lighting it up as she spoke.

'Imagine that you are in this tomb alone, Robin i' the Hood,' she spoke. 'The windows and doors are closed and locked. Flames start to creep up the tapestries.'

Robin paused, listening. This was not one his father had ever spoken of.

'Within seconds, the tomb is ablaze, and you will soon die, if not by the flames, then by the smoke,' Enna smiled widely, and Robin knew that she somehow also knew he didn't know the answer to this question. 'How do you escape?'

'Can the locks be broken?' he asked.

'No, the locks cannot be broken, and the flames cannot be put out.'

The wind was building up outside the room; a storm was approaching, and Robin was in the eye.

He didn't know the answer.

Desperately, he looked around the room, trying to think of a way out. There were no windows, the bricks were solid – he glanced at Nasir, impassive, stoic, simply waiting for the moment the game was over.

How would Nasir answer this? Robin thought to himself. Don't try to outthink this, you fool, be as Nasir would—

And just like that, the answer came to him.

'I would stop imagining,' he said.

The wind stopped abruptly; the flames, licking up the walls of the tomb were suddenly extinguished as Enna paused, staring in confusion at him.

'…what?'

'You said to imagine I was in a room filled with fire. To escape, I simply stop imagining this.'

Robin noticed Nasir's smile, as he nodded gently to himself.

'But that's not the answer,' Enna complained.

'But it's still a correct answer,' Robin placed his hand on the hilt of Albion, readying himself. 'And a promise is a promise.'

Slowly, he unsheathed the blade.

'So, I'll ask again,' he said calmly. 'Where is the grimoire?'

With a laugh, Enna told him.

10: The Trial of John Little

The following morning, the main square of Crow's Folly was filled to capacity; way more than the total sum of inhabitants of the village. Marion could only surmise that either news had come out about such a high-profile witch trial, and every surrounding village had emptied to come and see the show, or that Agnes Farrow had deliberately brought in her own crowd, people who would bay and cheer for blood.

Marion had hoped for the former, but as she walked with John to the raised cart in the middle of the square, the jeers and catcalls that came from the crowd showed this was way more likely to be the latter; Robin and his band of outlaws had helped almost every village in the surrounding countryside at some point, and Marion knew many of Crow's Folly who had items taken by the Sheriff, only to be returned days later, often by John himself.

And, unsurprisingly, many of those faces weren't visible in the crowd as John raised himself onto the cart, standing impassively amid the noise.

There was another cart, hastily turned into a stage opposite him. Agnes was now standing upon it, motioning to the crowd to silence but not pressing the point, allowing the noise to continue to help her cause.

Between the carts was a recent addition to the square, they had cut a tree down in the night and it now stood as a pyre, a pile of small sticks and tinder positioned around the base.

If it had ribbons from the top, it could have been a maypole, but Marion knew with a sense of dread exactly what it was.

It was the manner of John's execution if he failed to prove his innocence.

Clambering onto the cart beside John, Marion noticed he was staring directly at the pyre, as if daring it to attack.

'Are you ready for this, John?' she asked softly.

'As ready as I'll ever be,' John replied, and Marion could hear the defeat already in his voice.

Agnes, now boring of the jeers, finally motioned for the crowd to silence, and, looking over at John, she spoke, her voice loud to carry across the strangers.

'John Little of Hathersage, I accuse you of the gravest sorcery,' she intoned ominously.

'And he's innocent,' Marion replied, just as loud. Two could play at this game.

As the crowd murmured uncertainty at this, Agnes's smile widened.

'Do you have witnesses to attest to this claim?'

'Of course not. Do you?' Marion replied, and instantly regretted it. From Agnes's triumphant expression, Marion knew she'd walked right into the trap Agnes had prepared.

'Actually, yes,' Agnes replied, looking at one of the huts beside the square, guarded by two soldiers. 'Bring out the witnesses!'

There was a building of excitement as, from the hut, three villagers appeared. One was an old man, his white hair long and thin. The next was a woman, not as old as the man but still advanced in her years, her ruddy expression making her seem jolly, even though her face showed no joy being there. And the third, a young man with shaggy blond hair actively tried to escape the guards, before being pushed back to the side of the others.

'Who are they, John?' Marion whispered. John's expression was now one of sadness as he replied.

'That's Old Seth, I used to shepherd his flock,' he said, showing the old man. 'That's Mad Annie, she was our town's healer. The other, I'm not sure about. I think it could be Peter, the Miller's son, but he was a child when I left.'

Marion nodded. So they were Hathersage people, brought here specifically.

'And do any of them have a reason to hate you?'

John shrugged.

'Not that I know of. Seth and my da' were thicker than thieves. They'd do anything for each other.'

Marion watched the old man; she saw the fear, and more importantly the shame on his face.

This was not what she had hoped for.

'Then let's just hope that stays true from father to son,' she muttered, as she waited for the axe to fall on whatever plan Agnes had here. In response,

Agnes had the soldiers bring the old man onto the cart, forcing him to stand beside her.

'State your name,' she commanded.

'I'm Seth from Hathersage. Ma'am,' Old Seth replied nervously.

'And do you know the accused?'

'Oh, aye,' Old Seth replied with a slight smile, before realising where he was, the smile instantly flickering away. 'That is, I did.'

'Were you close?'

'He was like a son,' Old Seth nodded.

Agnes raised an eyebrow theatrically, performing for the crowd.

'And now?'

Old Seth swallowed, looked around, glanced at the soldiers, at Agnes and then John in succession, before looking at the floor of the cart.

'Now... Now I wish he were dead,' he breathed softly.

There was an intake of shock at this; Agnes waved it silent as she continued.

'And why is that?'

'Because he killed my flock,' Old Seth looked up at John as he said this, and there was anger and embarrassment in his eyes as he spoke.

The crowd, however, didn't see this and went wild at the accusation, howling with anger, gesticulating at John, who, in turn, shook his head in disbelief.

'That's a lie!' he objected. However, Agnes raised a hand to halt him.

'Quieten down, Little,' she hissed. 'Your friend there will have her chance to speak about this later.'

After a nod from Agnes to carry on, Old Seth cleared his throat a couple of times and then continued.

'The night after, well, the night after he joined the bloody Baron, he returned to the hut,' he said. 'Right out of his mind he was, all wide-eyed and frothing at the mouth. I thought he had some kind of plague.'

'What did you do?' Agnes ignored the horrified noises from the crowd, ignoring the villagers warding off evil with their fingers. Old Seth shrugged, looking around the crowd for support.

'Well, I didn't let him in, did I? Didn't want no plague in the house. The next morning I went out, and my sheep had been killed.'

'Killed? That's not the word you used earlier, when we spoke,' Agnes interrupted, holding Old Seth in her gaze until he relented, nodding.

'They were torn apart,' he revised.

Agnes smiled darkly as the crowd's noise grew at the words. Marion cursed under her breath. She was playing them for fools, and they were lapping up every word.

'And you know that John Little did this?' she asked.

'Well, he must have, yeah? I mean, when I heard of the other things he had done I knew it had to have been him,' Old Seth still sounded uncertain, still avoiding John's gaze. 'And if I'd let him in, I know he would have killed me and my Maggie too.'

As the crowd built up further in noise, Marion looked up at John.

'John!' she hissed. 'Say something!'

John shook his head instead, staring back at the makeshift pyre.

'Seth wouldn't lie. He really does believe I did that.'

He looked back at her, and for the first time, Marion saw the uncertainty in his eyes.

'What if I did, Marion?'

Marion patted his arm reassuringly, forcing a small smile onto her face.

'Well, let's hope that one of these three has something nice to say about you, or else we're in a lot of trouble,' she replied.

'You only just worked that out, have you?' John's voice was tinged with bitterness as he spat his reply. 'I was judged before this started. I reckon the only reason they sent Robin after that book was so that he couldn't stop this from happening.'

Marion nodded. She'd been thinking the same thing. Perhaps it was time to stop this one-sided show. Turning to the crowd, she called out, her voice cutting through the noise.

'Miss Farrow,' she said, her voice calm, condescending, as if scolding a child. 'I'm concerned here that you're not impartial. You stand in judgement of my friend, yet your witnesses all point to his guilt.'

'I'm not impartial at all! I want John Little to pay for his crimes!'

Whatever Agnes had expected, this was not it, as she spoke before she considered the implications. And, at the words, Marion smiled now, waving her hand around the square, playing to the crowd as much as Agnes Farrow had.

'Then how can you say this is a fair trial?' she cried out theatrically and was rewarded by a new murmuring of the crowd, as the undecided started to raise their concerns.

Agnes Farrow, however, simply smoothed her skirts, regaining her composure before replying.

'Because I'm not the one deciding this,' she explained. 'The judge will arrive tomorrow.'

This was news to Marion; nobody had said this before.

'Who?'

'The condemned man has no right here to demand such information,' Agnes sniffed, looking away. She was aware she was losing the crowd.

'He has a right to know who's holding his noose!' Marion protested again, louder this time.

'Next witness!' ignoring her, Agnes looked to the hut as she shouted, her voice cutting through the excited crowd. As she did so, John leaned over, speaking softly into Marion's ear.

'Marion, you need to get out of here,' he said.

'I'm not leaving you,' Marion placed her hands on her hips, shaking her head.

At this, John rolled his eyes in frustration.

'For God's sake! We don't know who's coming!' he hissed. 'It could be Gisburne or even the Sheriff!'

'Then we'll face them together,' Marion replied, unwavering.

'You think they'd respect that? You're an outlaw too! At least give Robin some notice!'

Marion was staring at Agnes now, trying to define some chink in her armour, something she could use.

'He can take care of himself. I'm staying, John. Whether you like it or not,' she said, absolutely sure of the words she spoke.

What she wasn't sure of, however, was whether the trial would still be ongoing by the time Robin returned…

11: Herne's Fate

After Enna had explained to them the location of the grimoire, Robin and Nasir had left Castle Belleme; the place was filled with memories for both men, neither of which were positive. Enna, in return for providing the information, had begged a boon of Robin; to kill Agnes Farrow, claiming the Baron would have wanted her dead. However, she wouldn't clarify the statement, retreating into the shadows, laughing maniacally, and so Robin had left without agreeing to the deal. And, later that morning, Robin had arrived back in the outlaw's camp in Sherwood to explain his predicament.

The problem was that John needed the book to prove his innocence, and Robin and Nasir needed to return quickly to Crow's Folly; however, the grimoire was in the possession of the Sheriff of Nottingham, held deep inside Nottingham Castle; a fool's errand if ever there was one.

But for John, no errand was too foolish.

The problem, however, was that on arrival the two men found the camp empty, with only Friar Tuck manning the fire, roasting what looked to be a hare on a spit. And, after explaining the issues, Robin considered his options: to wait for the others, staying close to Father Jonas and waiting hours – if not days – for the tax collector to arrive and take it from him (giving the priest plausible deniability when his flock's money was later returned). Or, to go it alone, at best with Nasir and Tuck for help.

There really wasn't a choice. The money Father Jonas would gain would feed a village, two even. John would be furious if he heard innocent people suffered just so they could free him.

Tuck wasn't happy about the prospects of a Nottingham break in, though, especially when he realised he would be one of the three people breaking in.

Tearing off a leg of the roast hare, Tuck chewed on it as he considered the options they had.

'How do we get in?' he asked through a half-filled mouth of juicy meat. 'Every time we find a way, they seal it up.'

'I'll think of something,' Robin mused as he paced, 'but before we do, I need to find Herne.'

'I'd better grab some supplies. A few days' food, perhaps,' Tuck was already making plans, but Robin stopped at this. Crow's Folly was less than a day's ride away, and the Castle was only a couple of hours.

'A few days?'

'Well, yes!' Tuck exclaimed. 'So that when they capture us and throw us in that pit, I don't starve!'

Gathering his longbow, and making sure Albion was secured to his hip, Robin laughed.

'You know, Tuck, that's what I love about you. Your boundless optimism,' he said. 'I'll speak to Herne, I'll work out what to do, and then we'll go get the grimoire.'

'Because it's always that simple,' Tuck moaned, tearing another strip of meat off the spit and chewing on it irritably.

'Save some of that,' Robin started to the edge of the clearing, nodding farewell to Nasir. 'You'll need it.'

'Will I?' Tuck looked at the leg in his hand. 'Why?'

'The pit,' Robin grinned as he left Tuck and Nasir behind. However, no sooner had he entered the greenwood, his smile fell, no longer needing to be faked onto his face.

For Robin had no clue how to do the things he needed. And his past was approaching, the ghosts were watching, and Herne had been strangely absent of late.

**

The punt was where it could always be found, and, stepping onto the narrow deck, Robin took the long pole and pushed off from the bank, heading across the lake, towards the cave and waterfall on the other side.

Through the waterfall, Robin steered the punt carefully along the narrow river, eventually opening out into an underground cavern, a sandy bank on the far end.

This was Herne's place. A place of power, of history, and of magic.

And, again, a place with no Herne the Hunter.

'Herne?' Robin cried out as he beached the punt, climbing out, pulling it up so the water wouldn't take it away. 'Are you here?'

With no answer, Robin walked over to the altar, beside the back wall of the cavern, whereupon a plinth was an ornate, carved wooden chest. Opening it, Robin felt a release of relief; the silver arrow was still there, held for when it was needed next. Holding it up, Robin—

'Well met, my son.'

The voice was close by and so unexpected that Robin almost dropped the arrow on the ground. Spinning around, Robin faced Herne the Hunter.

His ceremonial stag-head crown and leather cloak were absent, his old head covered now by a deer skin headpiece, his arms bare and tanned; but it was Herne, and suddenly Robin felt a wave of relief, a sense that things were going to be better now.

'You seem troubled,' Herne commented.

Robin swallowed.

'I thought you had left,' he said, wanting to explain more, but very aware that time was of the essence here. However, before he could say anything else, he stopped, staring past Herne, into the shadows of the cavern.

Ailric of Loxley once more stood there, half hidden in the darkness, wearing the same black armour as he had in Castle Belleme. Silently, he watched Robin, not even acknowledging him with a raise of a hand. Robin rubbed at his eyes, staring again.

Ailric was still there.

'Wait, am I hallucinating?' Robin asked. 'Herne – I swear I can see my father, faint but beside you.'

Without looking to see where Robin looked, Herne nodded, smiling faintly.

'You can,' he replied simply.

'How?'

Herne nodded to the ornate arrow in Robin's hand.

'The silver arrow you hold. While it is in your hand, the connection to the Otherworld is stronger.'

Arrow in hand, Robin walked past Herne, up to the shade of his father. He saw an expression of pride, and then sadness cross the shade's face as he looked upon his son, now a man.

'Father, I saw you in the forest, and in the castle,' he said. Ailric said nothing, although Herne spoke, as if for him.

'Yes,' he explained. 'At these times, he was merely a fleeting vision, though, trying to break through. All he could do was throw you breadcrumbs, lead you where you needed to go.'

'Enna,' Robin glanced back at Herne as he replied. In response, Herne nodded.

'My father isn't the only one I saw,' Robin added, once more feeling the shiver of ice slide down his spine. 'There's been others. Tom the Fletcher, and Dickon of Barnsley. I've seen them watching me from the woods. What does it mean?'

He stopped, forcing the next question out, softly.

'Am I to die soon?' he asked.

That the shade of Ailric shifted away, unable to look at him, worried Robin.

That Herne didn't reply immediately gave Robin the answer he didn't want to hear.

For it seemed that regardless of whether he saved John or not, Robin of Loxley would die.

12: The Hooded Man

After a long, uncomfortable wait, Herne finally looked back at Robin.

'You ask if you are to die,' he replied slowly. 'That is not for me to say.'

'If not you, then who?' Robin snapped, finally finished with the riddles as he spun to face the shade of Ailric. 'Father! Speak to me! Tell me if I'm going to die!'

Ailric's mouth opened and closed, as if he was trying to make sounds – but none came. Robin nodded, understanding. There was no way he would hear his father's voice once more. And, after the years apart, even Robin's own memories of his father's voice had altered; now every time he remembered a line spoke by Ailric during his childhood, it was almost as if his own voice spoke.

'Your father is proud of you, Robin,' Herne spoke for Ailric now, aware that Robin needed something, anything, from this. 'When he died, he knew that another Hooded Man would follow him. But he never believed that it would be you.'

Robin nodded, watching his father still, trying to fix every line, every crease in his father's face into his mind, aware that soon his father's shade might fade, and he would never see him again.

'How did you meet?' Robin asked.

'I came to him before the Saxon Uprising and offered him the silver arrow,' Herne smiled at the memory. 'He thought it was nothing more than folktales.'

'I only heard tavern tales, years later, about what happened to him,' Robin glanced back at Herne. 'How they found his body in the stone circle.'

Herne's face darkened as he spoke, and Robin felt the cavern move in upon him as the words echoed around it.

'The Sheriff's men killed your father. As they will one day kill you. This is the fate of Herne's Son.'

Robin nodded at this.

'I know. I've felt this for a while,' he sighed. 'I just hoped it would be longer.'

Herne moved closer now, placing a hand on Robin's arm.

'It would have been, but for your selfless action to save another,' he said.

Robin frowned at this.

'What action?'

'She lives because of it.'

Robin's eyes widened as he realised the implications of the words Herne spoke.

'Wait, you mean Marion? When I pulled the arrow out of her?'

Robin remembered the moment well; months earlier, King Richard had betrayed Robin's trust, and that night Guy of Gisburne had been sent to kill him, Marion, Tuck and Much. They'd escaped, but as they rode out of Nottingham Castle on two stolen horses, Marion behind Robin and Much behind Tuck, Guy, half-aflame from the blaze in the stables they'd escaped from, had loosed an arrow before he collapsed. They'd made it to the stones, the same stones that years earlier, Ailric of Loxley had been murdered within, and there they laid Marion to rest, her wound mortal.

But Robin hadn't accepted this, and had called upon Herne, using whatever power he had as Herne's Son, and Herne himself, or at least a vision of Herne had appeared in the circle, his arms outstretched, stating that the powers of light and darkness were with Robin, and ordering him to pull the bolt from her back. He'd done so, and with the ominous line 'the wheel turns', Herne had saved her life.

Or had he?

'She died, didn't she?' Robin whispered, half afraid to hear the truth.

'You pulled her back from the edge of death, but in the process gave of yourself, to return her life.'

Robin nodded. In a way, he knew this. He'd always known this.

'If I gave my life to keep her alive, it's a fair trade,' he smiled. And it was true, for even if he died, Marion would live. And that was everything to him. 'So what now?'

'There will always be a Hooded Man,' Herne replied, his voice soft, sorrowful even.

'Do you know when? When I die, that is?'

Herne shook his head.

'Do you at least know *how*?'

Herne nodded, and for a moment Robin thought he wouldn't reply. But then Herne sighed and spoke.

'When you too stand, like your father, with your quiver empty and your sword passed on,' he intoned. 'Herne's Son never dies. We become one with the trees, the land. Our memories live on forever.'

Robin took this in, nodding.

'Marion?'

'I will watch over her. She will survive.'

'Can you speak to her? Tell her she cannot grieve me?' Robin asked. 'If I must die, then she must live.'

Herne nodded.

'In time, she will find love once more.'

The phrase cut into Robin's heart; to learn that he could be so easily replaced was not a thing to hear, but at the same time, he would never had wanted Marion to live alone after he'd gone.

As if seeing Robin's dilemma, Herne looked down at the arrow, placing a hand on it.

'Marion of Leaford and Herne's Son, the Hooded Man, will always be linked,' he said. 'It is in the prophecies.'

'Good,' Robin looked away, back at Ailric. He remembered the last moments he had with him, when Ailric had sacrificed time, and most likely his escape, to ensure his son's survival.

We all sacrifice for those we love, he considered.

'Was this why you came?' Herne asked, and Robin felt the old man already knew the answer.

'No, I have a friend in trouble—'

'John Little.'

'Yes. Can you help?'

'No,' Herne shook his head, taking the silver arrow from Robin's hand. 'It is not my help that you need. It's the Sheriff. But I think your father knows a way of getting him to assist you. I can let him speak to you, this once, through the silver arrow.'

Robin looked over at Ailric, and for a moment the shade was more solid, more defined, as Robin's father finally smiled.

'Well met, my son,' Ailric of Loxley said.

***

It was another hour before Robin returned to the outlaw's camp; by this point, Tuck was almost apoplectic with worry, leaping up from the fire as Robin entered the clearing.

'About time!' he exclaimed, smiling widely at his friend's return. 'I was just about to start some dinner.'

As Tuck started humming to himself, walking back over to the pot that hung over the fire, Nasir rose from where he sat and walked over to Robin.

'You saw your father again,' he said, more a statement of fact than a question.

'Yes.'

'You spoke?'

Robin nodded.

'Through the silver arrow.'

Hearing this, Tuck almost dropped his ladle onto the floor.

'You spoke to your dead father? I'm not sure how I feel about that,' he admonished, making a cross with the ladle before continuing. 'What did he say?'

'Actually, he told me of a way into de Rainault's private quarters,' Unsheathing Albion, Robin crouched by the fire, warming his hands.

'Really? I thought we'd found them all?' Tuck replied.

'He suggested the front gate. As pilgrims.'

Tuck laughed at this.

'To pass as men of the cloth though, you'd need a real one to speak for...' his voice trailed off as realisation overtook his vocal cords. 'No. No, no, no.'

Robin stood up, slapping Tuck on the shoulder.

'You've got a couple of spare robes, right?' he asked.

The ladle forgotten, Tuck now wrung his hands together as he considered his options. 'What if I make a mistake? What if we get caught?'

Nasir, ever the diplomat, stared at him, stony-faced.

'Then you miss breakfast,' he said.

13: The Recess

The sun was setting by the time the third of the three witnesses had given their statements. It had not gone well.

John, in his defence, had weathered the storm on his character well; Marion would have expected lesser men to fall to their knees and beg forgiveness from the Lord, on some of the horrific tales that had been told of the possessed John Little.

No, Marion had to force herself to remember. The *lies* that had been told.

Agnes Farrow had presided over the trial like some mad queen; interrupting Marion when she protested some slanderous comment yet forcing Marion to wait when she herself did the same. Marion had willed herself to stay calm, to wait it out; she wasn't expecting to win, she just needed to keep John alive until Robin returned.

Although with a mysterious judge arriving the following day, Marion wasn't sure if she could manage that.

The day's entertainment finished, and the last witness escorted back to their hut, Agnes looked over to Marion, a vicious, triumphant smile upon her face.

'So, Lady Marion,' she mocked. 'You've heard three stories of John Little's horrors. Do you still wish to defend him?'

Folding her arms and setting her jaw, Marion stepped forward, as if daring Agnes to continue.

'I do.'

Interestingly, Agnes didn't respond, backing off slightly. It was as if Marion's unwavering defiance had shaken her somehow.

'Then we'll stop for the day, and restart tomorrow morning,' she muttered. 'You'll probably want an evening to prepare for what I'm sure will be a very thorough cross-examination.'

At this, Agnes turned and stormed off, the villagers also returning to their houses, or their carts and horses, realising the fun for the day was over.

The soldiers stood around the cart, waiting to escort John back to his hut, and Marion leant closer, gently tapping his arm to bring his attention back to her.

'Are you all right, John?'

As John glanced up at her, she almost recoiled; his eyes were haunted, the stories they had forced him to endure all day burning through to his soul. But even with all that, he still managed a weak smile.

'After hearing all that? Not really,' he whispered. 'I never thought I was an angel. I mean, when I came to, I'd been trying to kill Robin with a large stick. But I just assumed I'd been there for show, you know, to scare people into doing what the Baron wanted.'

He shuddered.

'Not… that.'

As the soldiers motioned for John and Marion to step off the cart and follow them, she replied, keeping her voice low.

'There's no proof, just witness accounts. And you don't know if Agnes has forced them into saying what they did,' she said, glancing back in case the woman in question was watching, but she was long gone, likely preparing for the following day's assault already.

'Peter said I killed his parents,' John snapped, tears forming in his eyes. 'They were my friends, Marion!'

'He also said that he wasn't there at the time.'

'What, so it could have been Nasir who killed them?' John shook his head, his anger rising. 'How does that make things better?'

Marion realised she didn't have an answer to this. In a weird, twisted way, John was right.

'Look. Get to safety,' John said as they entered the hut, the soldiers closing the door behind them, and taking sentry duty outside. 'I won't have you taken down with me.'

'Not this again—'

'I'm serious, Marion!' John's eyes blazed as he turned her to face him, gripping her arms. 'Go! I don't want you here! You're not helping!'

Marion pulled away, but didn't turn away, defiantly staring the larger man down. 'Nothing you say will make me leave,' she insisted. At this, John stormed over to the hearth, picking up the stick they'd used the previous night to poke the embers.

'What if I do something?' he waved it around the hut. 'What if I strike you with this stick?'

'You wouldn't. Because you're not the man they say you are. And I don't believe you ever were.'

John slumped down onto the stool, the stick tumbling to the floor as he placed his hands to his face.

'You don't know how hard this is for me, Marion. To let someone down is one thing, but to be told of the horrible things you did, and then have another tell you more – it's soul destroying,' he whispered, his voice hoarse and croaky. Marion walked over, picking up some wood and placing it into the heath, gathering some tinder as she spoke.

'I know,' she said. 'And that's why you need to fight. If only to delay the trial until help arrives.'

'You mean the Sheriff,' John rummaged around in his jerkin and pulled out some flint, passing it to Marion.

'We've escaped him before, we'll do it again,' she said as she struck the flint with the hilt of her dagger, the sparks igniting the tinder.

As she knelt down to blow on the small flame, John sighed.

'Right then. What next?'

Marion looked up from the hearth with a smile.

'You stop telling me to leave for a start.'

As a small fire burned in the hearth, Marion rose, sitting back onto the stool. John actually smiled; a small one but a smile, nevertheless.

'Done.'

Marion went to reply, but there was a faint tap-tap-tap at the window to the hut. It was narrow, not wide enough for more than a child to escape through, and so the soldiers hadn't considered it worth guarding, but at the same time there was still the slightest chance it could be someone looking to finish John Little before tomorrow's trial.

Or it could be Robin.

John picked up the stick once more, wielding it like a sword. He, too, had come to the same conclusion. Rising and walking to the window, dagger still in her hand, Marion stopped when she heard the soft, familiar female voice.

'John.'

John rose, confused.

'Rachel?'

Marion pulled aside the cloth curtain; there, on the other side, nervously glancing around, was Rachel.

'You've got some nerve coming here after what you did,' Marion snapped, and hadn't realised she'd brought the dagger up until John clasped one of his giant hands over hers, bringing it back down.

'It's okay, Marion,' he said before looking back at Rachel. 'You shouldn't be here, Rachel. If Agnes hears you've spoken to us—'

'To hell with Agnes Farrow!' Rachel spat out angrily, her voice rising. 'I can't live with myself any longer!'

'What do you mean?' asked Marion, dagger now sheathed.

Rachel looked around once more, still unsure whether or not she was being watched. Then, leaning forwards, hissed her next words into the hut, she uttered a conspiratorial whisper that changed everything for Marion and John.

'I mean Agnes Farrow isn't here for the reasons she says she is,' she hissed. 'And the people of Hathersage are under lock and key.'

John's face darkened, and the stick he held in his hand snapped with the pressure of his grip as it tightened.

'I think you'd better tell us everything,' he replied darkly.

14: Jerusalem Plague

The last rays of sunlight had long fallen behind the forest, as the final entrants to Nottingham Castle for the evening moved slowly through the main gate in single file, stopped under the giant portcullis as the guards checked their wares for contraband, or even worse – outlaws.

The Sheriff had given the order earlier that same day; there was a valuable item in the castle, and the last thing he wanted was the Hooded Man and his friends trying to steal it. And so now every single visitor to the castle had to pass through a customs check for their belongings.

To be honest, the guards were happy with this, as it gave them the opportunity to confiscate contraband items, or, rather, items they wanted for themselves. Already they'd gathered meat, cheese, some bracelets and a rather nice leather pouch, all taken with various excuses that, although usually ignored, were easier to enforce with the point of a sword.

'Move along!' they shouted; although the day had been profitable, it was drawing to a close and they had homes and taverns they wanted to get to. An old man with a sack approached, and the guards could smell fresh bread.

'Oi, what you got there?' one asked.

'Just some bread sir, for the market, tomorrow.'

'Give us a bit,' the other leant in, inhaling deeply.

'I only have—'

'Give us a bit or you stay out here tonight,' the first guard now unsheathed his sword menacingly.

Reluctantly, the old man gave a small loaf across.

'You're worse than the thieves,' he muttered as he walked through. The guards, munching on their stolen gains and hoping for some meat or cheese to go with it, looked up to the next in the line—

And stopped.

Ahead of them were three pilgrims; or, rather, two pilgrims, their heads covered with their hoods as they held them down in prayer, and a rather portly friar, standing at the front, all smiles.

'What do you want?' the first guard asked. Monks and pilgrims were notoriously poor; there would be no rich pickings here.

'I am a simple penitent, with my colleagues,' the friar continued to smile. 'We travel to the Nottingham Cathedral to gain God's mercy.'

'Mercy for what?'

The pilgrim behind the friar started to cough, a long, broken, cracking one that sounded like he was about to be sick right there and then. The guards couldn't help it; as one, they took a half step back as the friar, patting the coughing pilgrim's shoulder, looked back at them.

'Why, the Jerusalem plague, of course,' he said, gesturing back at the pilgrim with his thumb. 'Haven't you heard of it?'

'What sort of plague?' the guards hadn't. And the cough and the slight stagger of the weakened pilgrims had already unnerved them.

'First there's the cough, then the sweats, the boils... then madness and death,' the friar cheerfully explained. As he did so, the second pilgrim stumbled forward, catching himself, but then coughing hard onto the loaf of stolen bread.

'Oh, I'm so sorry. I'm sure he didn't mean to cough on your food like that,' the friar apologised. 'And we're almost sure he's not contagious, so you should be fine.'

At the word contagious, the guard tossed the bread at the friar, who expertly snagged it in his hand as they were waved quickly into the castle. The coughing pilgrims could be someone else's problem.

As the three travellers enter the cobbled streets of the castle's inner bailey, Robin leant in close to Tuck.

'Jerusalem plague? I thought you weren't allowed to lie?'

'Merely an embellishment,' Tuck shrugged, 'After all, you've been a plague upon the Sheriff for ages now, right? And Nasir came from there.'

Placing the purloined bread into the folds of his robe, Tuck then scrabbled around some more, pulling out his bible.

'What are you doing?' Robin hissed.

'I'm nervous, and that makes me hungry,' Tuck opened the bible, pulling out a small, round pie. 'Aha! Meat pie, anyone?'

'Where did you hide that?'

Tuck showed the book; some pages had been removed to create a nook within the bible, enough to hide a snack.

'There's a little place in my bible,' Tuck replied indignantly. 'What else am I going to read when we get caught and thrown into the pit?'

Robin stopped at a specific wooden door, opening it with a creak.

'I think you're focusing on the wrong things here, Tuck,' Robin waved for Tuck to enter.

'Isn't this the stairwell to the kitchens under de Rainault's rooms?' Tuck peered through. He knew the castle well.

Robin smiled.

'Oh, good,' Tuck sighed sarcastically, munching on his pie and entering.

***

By now, the night was drawing in, and the interior of the castle was lit by torches as Robin, Nasir, and Tuck slowly made their way up.

Robin stopped, however, as they reached a bend in the stairway. Peering around, he quickly slipped back against the wall.

'The Sheriff's door is guarded,' he hissed. 'Two men. We need a distraction. Tuck?'

Tuck sighed, raising his eyebrows.

'Again? You wouldn't ask me if I was dressed like Nasir.'

'True, but you're not,' Robin slapped Tuck's rump, motioning upwards. 'Off you go.'

Sighing, Tuck held his bible and pie in his hands, and walked up the stairs. He'd walked this route many times over the years; it was also the way to Marion's old room, but for the first time he felt like he was tresspassing.

'Oi, you,' one guard straightened as he passed.

Tuck stopped, swallowed, and turned slowly around. The last thing he wanted was for one guard to remember Marion's old confessor; the one that had run to the woods with the outlaws.

'Me?' he nervously replied, his voice quavering.

The guard pointed at the bible.

'Yeah, you. What you got there?'

'My bible?'

'The other thing.'

Tuck sighed.

'Oh, just a morsel of meat pie,' he held it up. At this, the guard's eyes widened, and he licked his lips.

'Meat pie? I ain't had that in ages,' he moved closer. 'Go on. Give us a bit. We've been stuck out here for hours.'

'Sheriff never feeds us either,' the other guard whined. 'We don't change shifts for ages!'

'Of course, my child. Here you go, take a piece,' Tuck smiled, holding out the pie. The two guards, focused on the food, didn't hear Robin and Nasir sneak up behind, nor did they see the hilts of the swords as they came down heavy on the backs of their necks. As the two guards fell to the floor, Robin pulled off his hood, looking around.

'Good work, Tuck,' he whispered, pulling the guards to the side, sitting them up. 'Tuck? Are you all right?'

Tuck stared at the two men, sighed, and then placed the pie on one's lap.

'It's the least I can do,' he moaned, reluctantly stepping away from it. 'As they said, the poor men don't get fed.'

Robin grinned.

'I'm sure the Sheriff will have some more to spare for you,' he said, turning back to the Sheriff's door, quietly turning it. 'Come on.'

Robin paused, his hand on the sturdy oak; this was possibly the craziest, most hare-brained thing he'd ever done. To break into the Sheriff's own bedroom, while he was likely in there...

John would do it for me, he reminded himself as he slowly pushed the oak door in and slipped into the room.

15: Robin Hood and the Sheriff

Even though the night was early, Robert de Rainault hadn't felt in the mood for carousing into the early hours of the morning, and had left the sycophants, the cronies, and the arguing Land Barons to their own devices, preferring to spend the evening in his chambers with a good book.

Or, rather, a bad book.

He'd been reading through the pages of the grimoire for most of the day now, and if he was brutally honest, much of what he'd read was woefully over his head. He was an intelligent, well-educated lord, and knew several languages, but much of this grimoire was written in Arabic; there were pages of nonsensical symbols and images, and if de Rainault was honest with himself, this wasn't the spell book he'd hoped for. The tales of sorcerers and witches told around tavern fires spoke of easy-to-read grimoires, with spells that rhymed. Not the dense, unfriendly prose of Baron de Belleme.

But no matter how much he wanted to throw it across the room, screaming, de Rainault believed that if he read it enough, if he examined the pages enough, he'd somehow magically understand it.

And there was the silver arrow. A page in the book held a detailed sketch of the cursed item; but the surrounding language was unknown. The Baron had constantly wanted it; he'd even sent in his own man to win it once, using his own dark magic to guide the arrows into the targets to get it.

But why?

What was de Rainault missing?

There was a soft rapping on the door to his chambers.

'Dammit! I said I wasn't to be disturbed!' he shouted out, and, as the door opened, he rose from his bed, wrapping his robe around him as he walked towards it, eager to release all of his grimoire-reading frustrations onto the poor soul who entered.

The man who entered, however, was not expected.

'I must have missed that order,' Robin said as he entered, with the Saracen, Nasir, and that portly friar following, closing the door behind them.

'Guards—' de Rainault shouted, but Robin held up a hand, halting him.

'I'm afraid the guards are a little distracted right now.'

'You killed them?'

'No, they'll wake with nothing more than sore heads,' Robin bolted the door as de Rainault backed into his room.

'So what is this,' he sneered. 'A kidnapping?'

Robin shook his head.

'More... a liberation,' he explained, pointing at the book upon the bed. 'That book you're holding, in fact. I assume it's the grimoire of Simon de Belleme?'

Moving swiftly, de Rainault blocked his path.

'And what if it is?'

'Then I need it to save a friend.'

At this, de Rainault smiled, finally understanding.

'Ah, you mean your "Little John",' he said, walking over to his side cabinet and pouring a goblet of wine. 'I'd heard about the trial. I've been invited to pass judgement on it tomorrow, in fact.'

Robin watched him carefully, expecting some sly attack at any moment.

'And what will you do?'

'I don't know,' de Rainault replied, waving his goblet, the wine sloshing within. 'I haven't heard all the facts of the matter. I do take my job very seriously, you know.'

'Yes. I've seen first-hand how seriously you take it.'

Ignoring the jibe, de Rainault paced around the room, envisioning the moment.

'I'll consider the facts, make a speech...'

He stopped, turning to face Robin – and smiled grimly.

'And then no matter the verdict, I'm going to burn your friend alive,' he said.

Robin resisted the urge to draw Albion and run the Sheriff through; he knew that this one death would bring forth hundreds in response.

'Give me the book, de Rainault,' he hissed.

de Rainault, however, had come to the same conclusion.

'Or what, you'll kill me? Don't make me laugh. An unarmed man in his bed? That'll really make the people follow you. Especially when Gisburne burns down villages in retaliation.'

'Robin, take the book and be done,' Nasir hissed, and de Rainault looked impressed. He didn't think he'd heard the man speak more than a handful of words. He'd assumed the man was incapable of speaking a civilised language. If only he wasn't outlaw scum, de Rainault might even ask him to translate some of the book, if he thought it would help.

The book.

'It won't work, you know,' de Rainault said, finally realising what was happening here. 'Giving her this book? It's what she wants.'

'What do you mean?' It was the friar that spoke.

'Wait, you haven't worked it out?' At Robin's confused expression, de Rainault laughed. 'The great Robin of the Hood doesn't know something, and I do? That's a rarity! Just bear with me a moment while I savour this.'

Robin stepped forward; the urgency clear on his face.

'Then help me understand,' he pleaded.

'Oh, I think not,' de Rainault shook his head, backing away again. 'I think I'll wait until Gisburne passes by, and then we'll see what happens.'

'He's right, Robin! We have to hurry!' The friar, always the coward, was glancing nervously at the door, and for a moment de Rainault wondered if the three of them would just leave. But Robin considered this for a moment and then shook his head.

'Tuck, Nasir, wait outside. Let me know if anyone else comes.'

'Robin—' Nasir started, but Robin patted his arm.

'I know what I'm doing, Nasir,' he said. 'Trust me.'

And with those two simple words, the friar and the Saracen unbarred the door and left Robin and de Rainault alone. As Robin re-secured the door, de Rainault watched him, suspiciously.

'Don't want your friends to see you murder me in my bed, then?' he asked.

'Actually, de Rainault, I'm going to make you a deal,' the outlaw replied, and with this, de Rainault poured himself another goblet of wine.

And then, on a whim, he poured a second, passing it to his hated enemy with a smile.

'I'm listening,' he said.

***

Sir Guy of Gisburne knew something was wrong from the moment the castle closed for the night. He'd heard guards talking of some mysterious Jerusalem Plague running through the castle, and the soldiers were restless. Something was going on, and added to that, the following morning they were heading to Crow's Folly to hang an outlaw.

'I want the horses readied for tomorrow morning,' he ordered his steward as they walked through the castle's corridors. 'We leave at sunup.'

'Yes, Sir Guy,' the steward nodded.

'And make sure my armour is ready. I'm expecting a fight,' Gisburne added. 'They won't let their friend burn. They'll try to save him. And I want to be ready when they do.'

He stopped, however, as he turned a corner; there, on the floor, were two sets of robes.

The type worn by monks, or pilgrims.

'Anyone seen the owners of these?' he asked, prodding them with his boot. The guards who spoke of the plague spoke of pilgrims. Were these the same people?

'I'm not sure, sire. Is it important?' One soldier, forgetting who he was talking to, voiced his opinion, instantly regretting it as Gisburne spun to face him.

'Oh, I don't know,' Gisburne mocked angrily. 'We could have two naked monks running around the castle, or we could have assassins here to kill the Sheriff! What do you think?'

He pulled his blade, staring up the stairs.

'You and you, come with me,' he ordered. 'The Sheriff's quarters are up there. We should make sure he's safe.'

'What if he's asleep, Sir Guy?' his steward asked nervously.

Gisburne leant in with a dark smile.

'Don't worry,' he cooed gently, sarcasm rife in his words. 'I'm sure he won't mind *you* waking him up.'

16: Pillow Talk

Robert de Rainault, the Sheriff of Nottingham and ruler of all that happened within his domain, chuckled at the situation he was currently in, staring at Robin of Loxley, Herne's Son, the Hooded Man, with a mixture of amusement and curiosity. It wasn't the first time he'd been in such a place, and the irony wasn't wasted on him.

'Tell me this deal of yours,' he waved his goblet at Robin, who'd rudely refused his own one, preferring to stand broodingly by the door.

'It's simple, really,' Robin explained. 'You let Tuck and Nasir take the grimoire and save John, and in return, you get me.'

'I get you?' de Rainault had to ask again, so sure was he that he'd misheard the offer.

'Yes, the moment my friends are safe.'

Narrowing his eyes, de Rainault pondered this for a moment.

'And what's to stop me from killing them, anyway?'

'It's not them you want,' Robin smiled.

'Not true. I want to kill you all.'

At this, Robin nodded, the smile still on his face. It irritated de Rainault.

'You like the chase more,' he replied, and the fact he knew de Rainault so well also irritated him.

'True,' he mused. 'And you'd just offer yourself to me? No wonder you didn't want them to hear you. What's the catch?'

He wasn't sure, but de Rainault was sure this question actually offended the outlaw.

'I'm not one of your Lords, de Rainault,' Robin spat. 'There isn't a catch.'

For a long moment, de Rainault examined Robin's face. There was something here that was unspoken, something he wasn't understanding.

'No, there's more to this than that,' he considered, walking back to his window. 'What aren't you telling me?'

There was a long moment of contemplative silence before Robin replied to this.

'Let's just say that I feel that my end days are approaching, and I want to ensure that they're not wasted.'

'And the silver arrow?'

Robin shook his head emphatically.

'That stays hidden.'

'Shame,' de Rainault watched Robin as he continued. 'Did I ever tell you how I gained it in the first place? The last 'Herne's Son' held it as my soldiers riddled him with arrows.'

Slowly, he approached, watching Robin's face.

'Ailric of Loxley, he was called. He was the Thane of the village, tried to start an uprising against me.'

'I've heard of him,' Robin replied calmly.

Of course you have, de Rainault thought to himself. You're from the same village, and you simple folk love nothing more than to gossip:

'I was young then, younger than Gisburne now,' he continued, his voice softening as he got lost in the memory. 'But I knew that there was something about him every time we faced each other. In a way, I respected him.'

'Yet still you killed him.' Again, the response was cold and calm. Icy, even.

'I'm Norman,' de Rainault shrugged. 'It's how we solve all of our issues. You remind me a lot of him, you know. Your face, your voice...'

'Is this going anywhere, or are you just reminiscing?' Robin snapped, the calm demeanour finally dropping. In return, de Rainault smiled triumphantly.

'He offered me a deal too, the day before he died,' he continued, and for a moment, the smile dropped.

He remembered the moment, and suddenly it made sense.

'His son's life for the arrow.'

'And what did you do?'

The conversation was soft, dark, and close now. Robin and de Rainault were locked together, and nothing would stop this truth from coming out.

'I burned his village down and took it by force,' he whispered. 'But I still let the child live, allowed him to grow up into a man. The man I now realise I see before me.'

67

Robin shook his head.

'I am Herne's son,' he breathed.

'Of course you are. Yet here you stand, offering me a similar deal. Your life for another's.'

At this, Robin snapped out of the spell, moving back, as if struck with a gauntlet.

'Will you take it?' he asked.

'No tricks?'

As Robin shook his head, de Rainault walked back to the bed, staring down at the grimoire.

'You know, Farrow summoned me because she thought my hatred of you would cloud my judgement,' he muttered, stroking the leather cover. 'All she really wants is this. Belleme's grimoire. Or rather, what's in it.'

As this, he opened the cover and, from a hidden recess within, pulled out a single piece of parchment.

I might not be able to read the blasted book, but I can read this, he thought to himself as he held it up, showing Robin.

'It seems that Agnes Farrow married Simon de Belleme before he left for the Crusades,' he smiled coldly. 'This is the certificate that proves it.'

'So this is about the lands and title?' Robin once more seemed appalled by this, and the Sheriff almost laughed.

Such a commoner way to think.

'Exactly,' he said, replacing the parchment. 'She probably heard that the Baron was dead, thought it safe to make a play. She knew I wouldn't give this to her, so she went to the next best thing.'

He turned back to Robin.

'You.'

'She played me.'

'Yes, she did, rather. But now it's placed me in a compromising position,' de Rainault sighed, sipping at his goblet. 'You see, I hate Agnes Farrow more than I hate you.'

'What, and the enemy of your enemy is your friend?'

'Let's not go that far. More a possible way to end her.'

Robin turned back to the door; faint, and through the wood he could hear shouting; soldiers had likely discovered Nasir and Tuck.

'Why do you hate her so?' he moved to the door.

'Do you have secrets you keep from the other outlaws?' de Rainault asked.

'Of course.'

'Would you tell me them?'

Robin turned back, torn between helping his friends or continuing this conversation.

'No.'

'Then don't expect me to do the same,' de Rainault pushed past Robin and unbolted the door. 'And it looks like our conversation is over, as your men have found Gisburne.'

With no resistance from Robin, de Rainault opened the door to find an out of breath and flustered Sir Guy of Gisburne at his threshold.

'My Lord!' Gisburne decried with glee. 'We've captured the Saracen and the friar—'

At this point, he saw Robin, and his sword rose once more.

'You!'

'Yes, yes, it's him,' de Rainault waved Gisburne to lower his blade once more, turning back to Robin. 'Drop your sword, Loxley, you're massively outnumbered.'

Nodding, Robin placed Albion gently on the ground, raising his hands.

'Shall I throw them in the pit?' Gisburne, realising something odd was happening here, and worried his fun was about to be ceased, enquired.

'No, I have a much better idea,' de Rainault replied, looking back at Robin. 'A far more permanent solution.'

17: Closing Statements

Marion wasn't surprised to see the crowds back the following morning; this was the second and final day of the witch trial, and by the end of it, they'd either see a man go free, a man they all knew, or they'd see a man burned alive.

Either way, they'd see something.

Marion wanted to shout at them, to scold them, but she couldn't. She'd seen so many trials and events over the year, and she knew better than anyone that people loved to see a little blood. And the higher your rank, the more blood you wanted to see, apparently.

Following their conversation the previous evening, however, Marion felt a little more prepared for this second day; for today she would be allowed to lead the questions, and John could speak.

'Are you ready?' she whispered to John, standing stoically on the cart beside her.

'I've never been more so,' he replied, and Marion could hear the anger in his voice, only just caught in check; he needed to hold it in until the right moment. 'Where's Rachel?'

'Left for Hathersage in the early hours of the morning,' Marion glanced at the other makeshift stage; Agnes Farrow had just arrived. 'She'll get there before Agnes's soldiers catch her.'

'Good,' John muttered as Agnes, now waving the crowd quiet, looked over at them.

'So, the final day has arrived,' she intoned sombrely. 'Does the accused have any last words to say? After all, the Sheriff will be here soon with his men.'

'Ah, so the Sheriff is the judge,' Marion smiled.

Agnes, however, frowned.

'You don't sound surprised.'

'Nothing you've done has surprised me,' Marion shrugged. 'And actually, John Little does have some final words to say.'

If Agnes was surprised at this, she hid it well, nodding as she stepped back, giving John the effective stage.

'Thank you,' he said, nervously clearing his throat. 'I'm not speaking to you with these words, I'm speaking to the people of Hathersage, the people that I'm accused of hurting.'

Turning, he sought the three witnesses who'd spoken against him the previous day. Finding them and seeing a couple of other familiar faces beside them, he continued, speaking from the heart.

'When I lived with you, I was a man with simple needs,' he started. 'I worked, I drank, I loved, I fought, but never with malice or evil in my heart. When the Baron Belleme took me, it wasn't by choice, and it wasn't without a fight. That I remember well.'

The crowd murmured at this, and John now turned his attention to them, too.

'But best me he did, and make me his man, he did. And as you've heard, I don't remember anything that happened afterwards,' he admitted. 'The things they say, that I attacked them, killed their livestock, their family, all of that, I can't tell you if I did those things, or if I didn't... as I simply have no memory of it whatsoever.'

Marion watched the crowd also, and what she saw emboldened her.

They were listening to John.

Agnes could also see this, and as she raised her hand to stop this, Marion stepped forward.

'Don't you dare,' she hissed. 'I am Marion of Leaford, and although I might not look it, I am more noble and of higher standing in any court in the land than you. And my friend will finish what he started; what you started.'

Agnes, thrown by the passion, stopped, and her pause allowed John to continue as he returned his gaze to his onetime friends.

'What I can talk about, though, is the man that I've been since,' he said, his voice rising in volume. 'Robin of Loxley freed me from this curse, a man that I'm grateful to call brother, and since that day I've done my best to atone for my past.'

He waved his hand over the crowd, knowing that every person there knew who Robin was, even if they didn't know the name 'Little John'.

71

'With Robin and other "outlaws", including Marion here, we've fought against injustice, helping the poor and the downtrodden stand up against their Norman overlords, finding them food and taxes when the Sheriff took everything they had, again and again,' he decried, his passion building. 'I am not the monster she claims I am! I stand with Robin the Hooded Man, the beacon of hope against the darkness!'

'Lies and fables!' Agnes, unable to stomach anymore shouted.

'It's true!' someone in the crowd, caught up in the moment, now shouted out. 'And everyone in Nottingham knows it!'

Nodding thanks to the stranger in the crowd, John looked over at Agnes.

'Aye, you can call me what you like,' he boomed. 'But don't call me liar.'

'Well, as illuminating as this all is—'

'I haven't finished yet!' John's thunderous voice, filled with fury, echoed around the village square. And, before Agnes could respond, John now turned his attention back to the crowd.

'You people of Crow's Folly, you've seen first-hand the help we've given the people of Sherwood,' he said, now pacing on the cart. 'All I hear in taverns are the stories of "Robin Hood" and "Little John", yet those tales are often as made up as the lies that this woman has told you about me. I'm not the monster she claims I am. I could never be that monster, and that is something I believe with all my heart, no matter how many "witnesses" I'm faced with.'

He took a deep breath, forcing his voice to stay calm, looking back at Marion, knowing that this was probably the most he'd spoken in one go in his entire life.

Nodding, smiling, Marion urged him to finish.

'But if I'm to die today, then I do it with pride in my heart,' he stated. 'Because if I've helped one person, if I've saved one life in my time on this earth, then I've made a difference. Do I have regrets? Of course I do. I'm sorry I never came home after, but I was ashamed, scared even.'

And now, at the very end of his speech, he turned the full anger of his gaze upon Agnes.

'But I'll be damned if I let a liar sully my reputation,' he hissed.

Almost as one, the crowd silenced at this. It seemed like even the birds stopped their noise, and the wind passing through the square was the only sound for a long, awkward moment.

'What did you say?' Agnes eventually managed to utter, in a half-choke of shock and anger.

'I said a *liar*, Farrow,' John repeated. 'These good people, these witnesses you bring here; did they come of their own free will?'

'Of course they did!' Agnes Farrow folded her arms, glancing at the soldiers, trying to work out what direction this trial was now taking, and how she could bring it back under control.

'Then why are their families under lock and key back at Hathersage?' Marion demanded. 'Are they kept hostage to ensure that your witnesses say what they're told?'

Agnes didn't deny this, now narrowing her eyes as she scanned the crowd.

'Who told you that?' she hissed.

'Rachel did,' Marion replied. 'Oh, don't go looking for her in the crowd, she's long gone, back to tell the Sheriff of Sheffield what you've done.'

'I did what God commanded me to!'

Now the crowd was murmuring again, but this time it wasn't in her favour. As Agnes looked around helplessly, Marion stabbed a finger at her.

'God commanded you to force innocent men and women to lie? To threaten their families?'

'You know nothing!' Agnes retaliated, her voice now rising in pitch and volume, as she saw her whole trial falling apart.

'Then let's ask the people that do,' John replied, glancing over at Old Seth. 'Your Maggie will be freed as soon as Rachel gets to her. And if she isn't, I'll make sure that Farrow never gets to her. All I want is the truth.'

The old man looked conflicted at this.

'I... My Maggie...'

'Would your Maggie want you to lie?' Marion stepped in now. 'To cause someone's death?'

'No, she wouldn't,' Old Seth nodded, and Marion saw his expression turn from worry into determination. But before he could continue, a villager to the south of the square shouted out.

'The Sheriff is here!'

And, in the distance, the flags of Robert de Rainault, Sheriff of Nottingham, could be seen approaching. As Agnes shrieked with triumph, Marion glanced over at John, and knew, with no doubt, that the expression of despair he wore on his face now would match her own.

For the Sheriff of Nottingham had arrived to give his judgement, and – for all his noble words in his impassioned speech – John Little was now damned to burn at the stake.

18: Judgement

As the procession entered the village, Marion could see de Rainault at the head, in his best livery, with Sir Guy of Gisburne to his right, a few steps behind, covered head to toe in his Norman armour.

Gisburne was armoured for a fight, she realised. He expects us to run. He's ready for a hunt.

Riding up to the centre of the village square, the villagers moving out of the way of his horse, de Rainault smiled at Agnes Farrow, as his men started fanning out around the crowd.

'Ah, Agnes. Looks like I'm here just in time,' he said, partly to her, but more as theatre to the village. As he spoke, Gisburne held off, moving back to the soldiers, his armoured helmet scanning the crowd, his eyes behind the slits narrow and searching.

'The crimes have been announced, the witnesses spoken,' Agnes gathered herself together. Where, but moments earlier everything had seemed lost, now there was victory in hand. 'Will you pass judgement?'

'That's not fair!' Marion stepped forward. 'He didn't hear any of it!'

At this, de Rainault actually nodded, smiling at Marion, giving her the instant impression that something was terribly wrong here.

'You're right, Lady Marion,' he nodded his head to her. 'It's only fair I hear some of this.'

He looked down to Old Seth.

'Are you one of the witnesses?'

'Yes, sir.'

Still smiling, de Rainault looked over at Agnes.

'What's he a witness of, exactly?'

'John Little killed his livestock and almost killed his family.'

At this, de Rainault raised his eyebrows in mock shock, looking back at the old man.

'And is this true?'

Old Seth looked up at the Sheriff of Nottingham, then to John, and then to Agnes before shaking his head.

'…No, sire,' he replied.

As Agnes started to purple, and the watching crowd cheered, de Rainault looked to the next witness, Peter.

'And you?'

'He's accused of killing my parents while under Belleme's spell.'

'And did he?' de Rainault stared at Agnes, holding her gaze as he spoke to Peter, who looked to the ground, ashamed.

'No. They're still alive.'

'Lies!' Agnes Farrow screamed. 'Take him to the stocks!'

'Belay that order or my men will cut you down where you stand!'

As his own men raised their weapons, de Rainault returned to Agnes, now white-faced and terrified.

'I just do my job, Sheriff,' she whispered.

'No, Agnes,' he replied sadly. 'You look for Belleme's grimoire.'

'Only for proof! They claim he was bewitched!'

'Well then, we'd better check,' de Rainault looked back at his procession, nodding to a steward, now holding an ornate leather book in his hands. 'Take the book to the Witch Finder.'

Snatching it from the steward's grasp, Agnes now flicked through it eagerly, as if looking for the proof she needed. However, watching her, de Rainault narrowed his eyes.

'That's it, have a good look through,' he said, his voice as cold as ice. 'I'm sure you'll find what you're looking for. As it goes, I have a witness of my own.'

Looking up from the grimoire suspiciously, Agnes frowned.

'What do you mean?' she cautiously asked, her eyes narrowing.

'Someone who knows why you wanted that book so badly,' de Rainault looked back to Gisburne, who, at a nod, pulled off his helmet to elicit a gasp of shock from the crowd, Marion and John.

'I'm sorry it took so long to get back to you,' Robin smiled, tossing the helmet to the side, 'but as you knew already, the Sheriff had the book.'

'Where is it!' Agnes shouted, and at this, suddenly remembering, Robin pulled a sheet of parchment out from under his tunic.

'Oh, you mean this piece of paper?' he smiled.

'It's mine!'

'And yet I hold it,' Robin replied, his voice filled with bitter anger as he looked at the crowd, holding the paper up. 'This is the wedding decree of Agnes Farrow and Simon de Belleme, at Whitby Abbey, before the Baron went to the Crusades. But it was kept secret.'

Agnes slumped, defeated.

'Because he was betrothed to another,' she muttered sadly. 'He promised to tell her before he sailed.'

'But he didn't, did he,' Robin climbed from his horse now, pulling off Gisburne's tabard, revealing his own forester's green underneath. 'And when he came back, years later, he was a changed man. He was a slave to the Dark Lord Azael.'

'He didn't even recognise me!' Agnes spat, no longer caring who heard. 'He returned to tell me we were never married. He tried to kill me, and after I escaped, the nuns at Whitby nursed me.'

'And then you became a Witch Hunter,' Marion leant against the edge of the cart as she mocked her. 'Poor you.'

'He deserved to pay! They all did!' Agnes was frothing now, and Marion couldn't deny that she was enjoying this a little.

After all, the Sheriff would soon capture and likely execute them soon, so why not enjoy things right now?

'So when did you learn that the paper still existed?' pulling Marion out of her thoughts, de Rainault was now facing Agnes once more.

'Recently. I witch-tried a woman, Lilith,' she replied. 'She claimed she recognised me, used it to beg for her life.'

Robin stepped forward now, and Marion saw the flash of anger cross his eyes. Lilith had been the one that enchanted him, that raised Baron de Belleme with him. They thought she had escaped and was now with the Baron.

'What happened to her?' he demanded.

Agnes spat on the floor.

'Justice,' she hissed, and Marion felt a pang of regret fizz through her. Lilith had done terrible things, but the trial she would have had was likely to have been as much a sham as this one.

Unaware of the information she'd passed, Agnes pointed once more at the parchment in Robin's hand.

'That paper proves I am the rightful ruler of Castle Belleme and all its property,' she declared furiously. 'I am the Lady Belleme and I now demand my dowry!'

The crowd went quiet on this; many of the villagers, having come from simple lives, didn't understand what was actually going on here, and those that did were rapidly realising that the trial was going in a very different and dark direction now.

At Agnes's outburst, de Rainault checked his fingernails before buffing them on his surcoat.

'About that,' he said genially. 'Unfortunately, only I can confirm that upon you.'

He looked at Robin, holding out his hand. Nodding, Robin walked to his horse, passing the manuscript to the Sheriff of Nottingham, before stepping back.

As they did this, Marion walked back to John, whispering into his ear.

'I can see Nasir by the woods,' she said, indicating with her eyes down one lane, the fields and the woodlands on the other side of them empty. 'He waved to me before disappearing.'

'Aye,' John replied softly. 'And Will is across the other way. I saw him but a moment ago. They're waiting for something; I hope Robin knows what he's doing.'

Marion agreed to this as de Rainault, now examining the parchment, looked up at Agnes.

'So you were willing to burn this man at the stake to get this back?' he sneered. 'That's truly a dark act. Not the act of the woman I once knew.'

'That woman died when you left her at the altar!' Agnes shouted back, and Marion glanced across at Robin. As their eyes met, both could see the surprise at this revelation. Neither had known of the Sheriff's onetime love with the Witch Hunter.

If the revelation shook de Rainault, he didn't show it; sniffing, looking up the sky, as if seeking divine guidance, and then looking back down at the stunned crowd, he milked the moment for all he could, before replying to the crowd rather than Agnes, slowly riding towards the pyre, and the flaming torch beside it.

'I think you'll find it was the other way around, but yes, I suppose she did,' he admitted. 'But to destroy a life through fire? That's more my line of work.'

Now within reach of the torch, de Rainault held the parchment out above it, allowing the flames to lick at the edges, ignoring Agnes, now trying to clamber onto the pyre itself, to snatch the paper from him.

Please, no!

'You don't want this, Agnes,' de Rainault said as the parchment and legal document written upon it burst into flames. He let go, allowing it to fall into the pyre. 'It's tainted with dark sorcery. And we all know how you hate that.'

As Agnes Farrow fell to her knees, scrabbling through the tinder beneath the pyre, trying to salvage the last of the document, de Rainault turned his attention back to John.

'John Little, you're cleared of witchcraft and sorcery,' he said to the cheers of the villagers watching. 'But… you're still an outlaw.'

Marion felt her heart plummet as the Sheriff looked to his entourage.

'Guards!' he ordered, and as one, they drew their weapons.

Seeing this, Robin stepped forwards.

'What are you doing?' he shouted in anger. 'We had a deal!'

As the guards moved in on John, Marion, and Robin, de Rainault smiled widely as he looked down at his nemesis.

'I'd be a poor guardian of the law if I allowed three of the most heinous criminals in Sherwood to just walk away,' he replied, holding his hands piously together as he spoke, before shouting to his commander.

'Find a sturdy tree,' he ordered.

'We're hanging some wolfsheads today.'

19: Nothing Is Forgotten

As Robin glared up at the Sheriff, de Rainault gave a pained expression, as if realising the poor, simple man had misread something very important.

'You didn't actually think that I would uphold my end of it, did you?' he asked with mock concern.

Robin, however, simply smiled widely. A smile that instantly filled de Rainault with genuine concern now; the outlaw knew something he didn't, had made a move he hadn't expected. But what was it?

'Not really,' Robin replied, stepping back from the soldiers. 'But then again, did you really think I would do the same?'

Before de Rainault could say anything, Robin tucked two fingers into his mouth and blew a shrill whistle. As he did so, three arrows slammed into the pyre, immediately beside him, each from a different direction, his horse jerking back with fright.

'You shouldn't have let Nasir and Tuck go,' Robin said, calmer than he should be as he addressed the crowd.

'The Sheriff has possibly been possessed by de Belleme's grimoire!' he cried out. 'He doesn't know what he does, just like John Little didn't.'

'Don't be a fool,' de Rainault snapped. 'I'm fine.'

However, as he glanced at his men, he saw concern and fear on their faces, as Robin continued, climbing onto the cart beside John and Marion as he did so.

'But fear not, because as you all heard when I was here before, the Witch Finder there begged me to find the truth, to find the sorcerer.'

He looked at de Rainault, and his eyes glittered.

'So, as I kept him busy, my men raised an army of god-fearing people to banish the fowl demon within him,' he said. 'To the north, led by Will Scarlet, are fifty villagers. To the south, led by Nasir, are fifty more, with horse and bow.'

He walked to de Rainault now; the cart giving him the height to stare at the Sheriff eye to eye.

'I also have men to the west with Much,' he breathed. 'You're boxed in and seriously outnumbered. Do you really want this fight? You've beaten Farrow.'

He leant in.

'Take the win.'

'You're lying,' de Rainault hissed.

'About what?' Robin replied. 'The numbers? Or your demonic possession?'

He nodded at the Sheriff's guard, nervously looking around.

'At their best, it'd be a fight,' he whispered. 'Like that...'

'Fine! Get out of here!' wheeling his horse around and riding from the cart, de Rainault hissed out his response. 'All of you!'

'Appreciated, Sheriff,' Robin said, already jumping to the ground, helping Marion to the grass. However, de Rainault climbed off his horse now, passing it to his steward as he walked back to Robin. His sword was sheathed, but he had murder in his eyes.

'But know this, Loxley,' he hissed. 'When I finally end you, I want you on your knees, bloodied and broken, hunted down and with the silver arrow in your hand.'

Now it was de Rainault's turn to lean in close.

'The silver arrow that you will give me willingly.'

Robin stared at the Sheriff for a long moment, envisioning this future encounter in his mind. Eventually, his clouded eyes cleared, and he nodded.

'That will never happen,' he said, grabbing Marion and, with a nod to John, leading the two outlaws out of the village and towards the woods to the north.

Robert de Rainault, Sheriff of Nottingham, glared after them.

'We'll see,' he hissed, now looking back at Agnes, the tattered and useless burnt remains of her marriage documents in her hand.

'And what about me?' she demanded.

'There's no crime for being a zealot to the cause,' de Rainault replied. 'And thanks to those charred pieces of paper, this is the only cause you have left.'

'I shall go to London! King John will hear of this! That you let the Hooded Man go!'

At this threat, de Rainault simply smiled.

'And I'm sure he'll shout and snarl and send someone to me, claiming that my head will be on a plate if I don't capture him,' he sighed. 'It's not the first time, and it won't be the last. I'm sure one day I'll lose this job, but it won't be you that ends it.'

He looked around the now emptying village square. Walking to the cart on which she had until recently stood, he leant across and picked up the discarded grimoire, walking back to his horse.

'Oh, and take your guards with you when you travel to London,' he advised sternly, climbing back onto it. 'Travelling through Sherwood is dangerous, so I hear. Now get out of here, my love.'

***

Of course, there hadn't been a hundred and fifty eager villagers surrounding them, just Will, Much and Nasir with bows; but Robin had little time to prepare, and to be honest, it had amazed him it even worked.

And now, walking back to their camp in Sherwood, the air was rife with laughter, the success of yet another tryst with the Sheriff, another where he lost while the outlaws won, sitting sweetly on their lips.

'I can't believe you tried to make a deal with the Sheriff!' John admonished Robin as they walked.

'Neither can I, John!' Will laughed, punching John's ribs. 'Especially for you!'

'Well, I for one am glad he did,' Much interjected. Will, realising Much hadn't realised it was a joke, patted him on the back.

'Ahh, come on, Much. I was only joking,' he said, before pausing, an idea coming to him. 'Maybe we should have given you in place of him?'

'You wouldn't!' Much exclaimed, looking around in horror as the others laughed. 'Why would you even say that?'

'Much, it seems I need to teach you what a sense of humour is,' Will placed a brotherly arm around his friend.

'You'd have to find your own first!' Much replied to the other's laughter, finally getting – and getting in on – the joke.

As they continued to walk, Marion slid up next to Robin, whispering.

'And the ghosts, Robin?'

Robin shook his head.

'Laid to rest.'

'Good,' Marion nodded. 'And all that talk of dying?'

There was a flicker, a pause before Robin replied, the faintest of reassuring smiles on his face as he spoke.

'Nothing but scary stories for the campfire,' he said, quickly changing the subject. 'Come on, we need to get back to the camp before Tuck eats the whole pie.'

'Wait. Pie? What pie?'

Robin laughed.

'He stole it from the Sheriff's own pantry! Claimed it was recompense for the piece he lost!'

As the conversation turned to pies and the acquisition of such things, Nasir slowed down until he walked beside John, a small way back from the others.

'You look troubled,' he said.

'Nah, I'm fine, Nasir,' John replied with a smile as weak as Robin's had been.

'I am not them,' Nasir nodded at the others, laughing and joking. 'I was there. You can talk to me.'

'I know. And when the time comes, I will, I promise,' John replied, before adding, 'one thing. Do you remember anything about that time?'

'No,' Nasir's response was concise.

'And it doesn't worry you? That you don't know how many you killed?'

'No.'

John paused, staring at his friend. Seeing John's confusion, Nasir hunted for a way to explain.

'It was not me,' he said. 'As it was not you. You are imagining the worst things possible.'

'Aye. But how do I stop that?'

Nasir shrugged.

'You stop imagining.'

'Heh. How did you get so smart?' John laughed as they started walking again.

Nasir smiled.

'I stand with people like you.'

John frowned.

'I don't know if that's a compliment or an insult,' he said before shouting out to the group in front. 'Hey Robin, has that taxman collected from Father Jonas yet?'

Robin looked over at Much, who paled.

'You called me away,' he said defensively.

'Well, then I'm going to get the blame if he has,' Robin sighed. 'Come on, let's grab Tuck and make our way there.'

'You can't always be everywhere, Robin,' Much complained. 'That's the trouble.'

'Never fear, Much,' Robin placed his hand on Much's shoulder. 'You're my oldest friend, and my brother, if not by blood. Wherever there's trouble, I'll be there.'

'With us?'

Robin embraced Much as he smiled.

'I'll always be with you.'

'You promise, Robin?'

Robin's voice faltered; with what he knew, this was a promise he couldn't make. And looking across at Marion, watching him, smiling, caught up in the moment, he knew he could tell no one what he now knew.

Soon, very soon, in fact, he would likely die at the hands of the Sheriff. And, when he did, he would return to the forest, like Tom, Dickon, even his father, Ailric of Loxley, and a new guardian would appear to take on Herne's Hooded Man mantel.

Robin didn't envy them, yet at the same time was jealous of them; jealous of the adventures they would have, the friendships they would make, the love they would receive.

Herne's prophecy echoed through his head once more as he stared at Marion, aching with the love he had for her. Love that had saved her life at the expense, it seemed, of his own.

In time, she will find love once more. Marion of Leaford and Herne's Son, the Hooded Man, will always be linked.

Robin looked back at Much, forcing a final, bittersweet smile.

'I promise, Much. Herne's Son will never die,' he said.

And as Robin of Loxley, the Hooded Man and current Herne's Son led his friends back to their camp, still laughing about pies, the ghosts of Sherwood Forest that had followed him dissipated into the trees, the ancient forest at peace once more.

~

Also Available

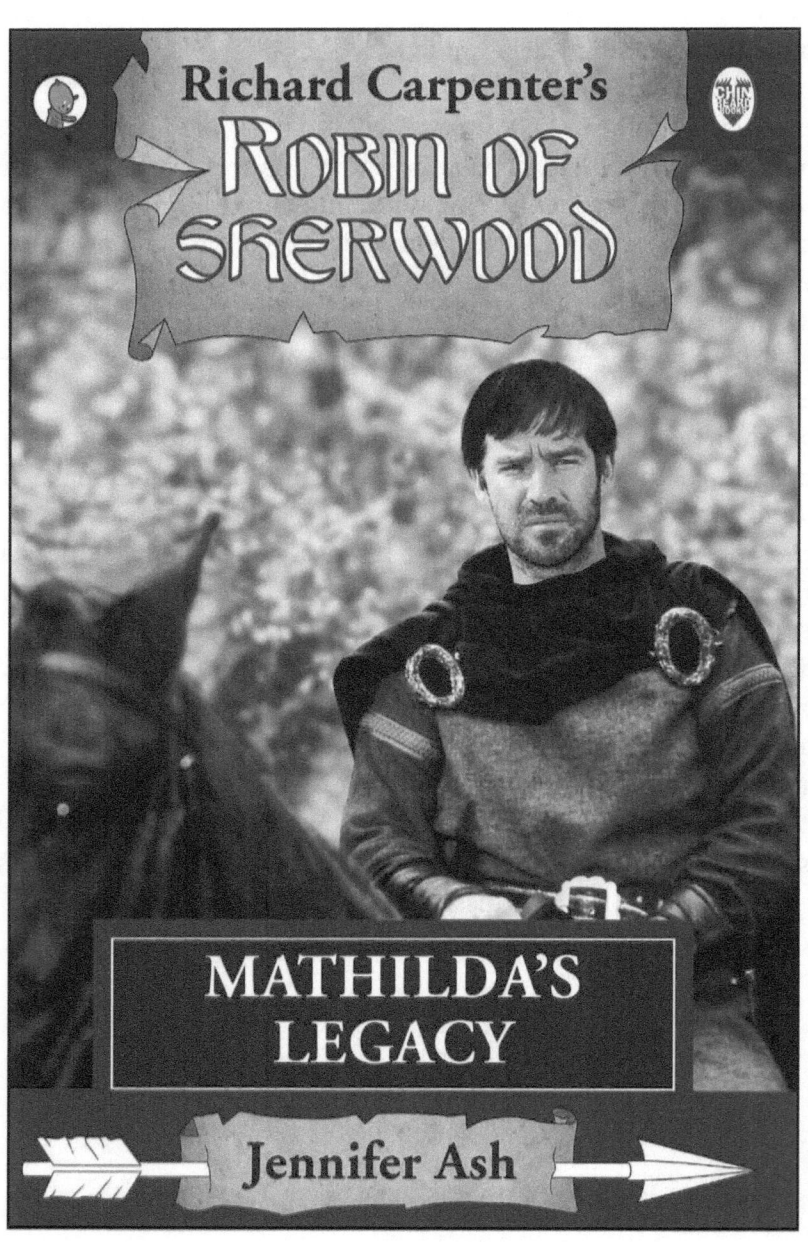

Richard Carpenter's

ROBIN OF SHERWOOD

MATHILDA'S LEGACY

Jennifer Ash

www.ingramcontent.com/pod-product-compliance
Lightning Source LLC
Chambersburg PA
CBHW022047170626
46808CB00003B/1391